TAYLOR'S LAND

PETE KOSKY

Mountain State Press
MOUNTAINSTATEPRESS.ORG

HUNTINGTON • 2024

ISBN: 978-1-7351635-4-3

Cover art: Andrea Sinclair
Book design and interior: Mark Phillips

Copyedited by: Sophia Dodson, Eden Norris, Mikayla Steele

Edited by: Cat Pleska

Mountain
State Press
MOUNTAINSTATEPRESS.ORG

mountainstatepress.org
In collaboration with Marshall University

DEDICATION

*To Early Vermillion for forty years
of repairing my guitars and banjos.*

Books by Pete Kosky
published by Mountain State Press

Mountain Tales & River Stories
Mountain Tales II

ACKNOWLEDGMENTS

Though I am the author of this book, it is truly a group effort to get a book published. I am grateful to Cat Pleska of Mountain State Press not only for publishing this book but for being an early advocate and promoter of my writing. I sincerely appreciate, and am thankful for, her continued support, hard work, and friendship. Cat, along with Kirk Judd, encouraged me to join West Virginia Writers and thanks to them I feel very welcome in the West Virginia writing community. I would also like to express my gratitude to John Blisard, Kirk Judd, Bob Maslowski, Cyrena Parsons, and Mack Samples for taking the time to read the early draft and provide constructive criticism and further encouragement to continue. They are all trusted friends whose input helped to make this a better book. Also, a special thanks to my patient wife Ariana for taking the time to proofread and silently improve my spelling and grammar.

CONTENTS

Prologue: Death in the Quiet Zone

The mountains in the evening twilight went
from distant dark silhouettes across rolling fields and
meadows to giant walls of thick foliage and tree trunks.
The foliage softly reflected in the headlights of the station
wagon as it sped along Route 219 over an hour north
of Lewisburg. She was heading home with a car full of
groceries after making her monthly journey south to
Walmart. It was just under four hours round trip, but still
closer than going to Elkins. The local Food-Fair was fine
for small commodities, but for bulk items, it was worth
the aggravation of a long drive.

She had gotten a late start that day and as a result
ended up having to drive home just at dark, something
she had wished to avoid. The two-lane was full of curves
and switchbacks, last winter's potholes, steep inclines,
high ridgelines, and deep valleys. She used the high
beams for as much of the trip as possible, ready to brake

if necessary. She watched for patches of fog or deer in the road. The cool mountain air of summertime blew in through the open windows when the horizon exploded for a split second with a flash of lightning that lit up the barren countryside. An ominous peal of rolling thunder immediately followed as the windshield was suddenly pounded with millions of raindrops that hit the glass like tiny translucent nails. She was half-soaked as she furiously worked to crank up the driver's side window; the passenger side would have to wait until later. She grabbed her purse and shifted it from the passenger side to the back seat among bags of groceries to keep it dry. The rain was so violent that she searched for a wide spot on the road to park for a while until it passed.

A minute later she was parked just off the road and, with the passenger window rolled back up, intended to wait out the storm. The noise from the rain was deafening as she shifted the seat back a notch to make herself more comfortable. She threw her purse back onto the passenger seat and for a moment wished that she had a cell, but cell phones were useless in the Quiet Zone, the large area of West Virginia where cell service was not available due to its proximity to the National Radio Observatory in Green Bank. In general, this was not a big problem for her, but in situations like this she just wished she had service. She had left the baby with her mother, and it would have been nice to be able to check in on him.

The rain had slowed up just a touch when bright beams of light shot through her rear window and harshly reflected in her rearview mirror. A vehicle had pulled up directly behind hers, a large frame truck with windows set much higher than her station wagon. Through the din of the pounding rain, she heard the muffled thud-like sound of two doors slamming shut. A man tried to jerk open the driver's side door a second after her gut told her to hit the lock. Then the passenger door, which was not locked, was thrown open by another man. Crazed laughter, desperate screams, and driving rain soon filled the front seat. Later, all she could remember was the smell of cigarettes, whisky, sweat, body odor, and the blur of faces disfigured by the darkness as dirty wet hands attacked her from all sides.

She was found the next morning by a passing motorist who drove her to the nearest town, who discovered she was in shock. County Deputies and then the State Police were notified. They were able to establish that she had been sexually assaulted, beaten, and robbed. Her purse had been emptied and jewelry stolen. She was not able to identify her attackers in the dark. Hers was the first of several such attacks that took place that year along Route 219, north of Lewisburg. Unlike the others, at least she had lived.

Chapter 1. Taylor Meadows

Like many other unincorporated small towns in West Virginia, Taylor Meadows was little more than a quiet crossroads to most travelers. A reflective metal sign standing on the berm of a narrow two-lane road off Route 219 announced its existence, and it seemed to suddenly pop up from the dense woodland as one headed down the mountain. For the tourist it appeared that one was in the forest one minute and then in this cleared little valley the next. The noise and speed of an automobile passing through were in deep contrast to the quiet peace and slow pace of the settlement. The fresh mountain air was augmented with the scent of new-mown hay and, in the cooler months, wood smoke. Clean farms; neat houses with yards that set back off the road, many with large, covered porches with lots of hanging plants and homemade lawn ornaments. In some ways it appeared to be a portal into the past. The core of

the town clung to either side of the main road. Passing
on through, the farmland disappeared and the dark
forest reclaimed the road.

The mountains surrounding the town were a
lush, impenetrable green in summer and painted with
breathtaking brightness in the fall. By early October, the
brown fields gazed up in wonder at the speckled mixture
of red, yellow, and orange leaves at their peak of color. A
month later a new generation of fallen leaves carpeted
the fields at the edge of the woodline and blanketed the
forest floor, leaving the distant ridges dark brown against
the stark blue skies of early winter.

Originally a small frontier settlement, the
crossroads grew exponentially for several years during
the great logging boom in the early 1900s. The more
loggers came to the region, the more timber was cut
and shipped out. When the boom ended in 1920, it was
as if the mountains themselves heaved a great sigh of
relief, and the wood hick settlements and logging towns
seemed to deflate like a tractor tire with a slow leak.
Those who were left behind picked up the pieces and
carried on; they were proud of their mountain heritage
yet forever aware of how their people and mountains
had been used for the gain of outsiders.

Just as the smallest part of an iceberg is the part that appears to be floating on the surface of the ocean, and the largest part is unseen below the waterline, so it was at Taylor Meadows. Most of the people and farms were not visible from the road. What the tourists saw was only a sample. And just like an iceberg, the most dangerous part is hidden from view.

Chapter 2. The Home Place

The land surrounding Jolly Taylor's farm had a tired, used-up look to it, not unlike a faded flannel shirt. While the rugged karst limestone landscape was beauty itself in the eyes of some, it was pure desolation to others. Those who favored it, like Jolly, were content to wear the land like an old flannel shirt no matter how threadbare or worn. Others cast off the ragged garment to seek more modern attire in faraway places outside of the region. Those who left were often gone for good; those who chose to stay felt the powerful draw of deep-seated family roots and an internal love of the land too strong to overcome.

Jolly had lived on or near his family farm for nearly all his 62 years. With the passing of his mother over ten years ago he had inherited the home place and taken over the small farm that had been in the family for over six generations. The nearby town of Taylor Meadows was named for one of Jolly's forebears, as was Taylor Notch State Park where Jolly worked as custodian and handyman.

Where his ancestors fought Indians, cleared fields, built homesteads, and raised families, he made sure the park's outhouses were filled with toilet paper, cut firewood, and cleared roadkill off the blacktop. Where homesteaders once relied on a Taylor to help build a cabin, skin an elk, or harvest the crops, now D.C. patricians who camped in the park regarded Jolly as their personal servant whose lineage and ties to the land meant nothing. To most of them, he was just the guy with the chainsaw in his pickup. He always waved and smiled from his 1996 Toyota as the Land Rovers and other high-end SUVs passed as they exited the park, for that was the only time he liked them—when they were leaving. Jolly considered himself lucky to have his job as a park attendant, for jobs were hard to come by in the county. He was also able to add a special sense of personal pride to his work at the park, for it not only carried his family name but was also built partially by a family member.

Jolly's uncle Jess was a young, newly recruited member of the Civilian Conservation Corps when he

was assigned to help build Taylor Notch State Park in
the late 1930s. Jolly often thought about the stories his
uncle had told him about the CCC and the park itself.
His best recollection was when he was able to attend
a small reunion of several of Uncle Jess's CCC buddies
for the park's fortieth year in 1976 while home on leave
from the army. Jess had worked the park-issued charcoal
grill while the old-timers sat under one of the sprawling
pavilions they had built with their own hands so many
years before. Canned beer, cigarettes, and good-natured
laughter fueled the seemingly endless stories that day,
and Jolly listened as hard as he could, dedicating them
all to memory.

The best stories were not about the particulars of
the physical building of the park, but rather of the off
time. Jolly could still see the twinkle in his uncle's eyes
and hear his raspy recollection as he waved a cigarette
through the air for emphasis, talking to Jolly as much as
to the others. He remembered one story vividly:

"You know we only got a dollar a day for that work.
Come payday they gave us five dollars cash and they sent
the rest home. Well, five dollars back then was worth pert
near seventy or so dollars in today's money, so we could
do a lot of damage when we hit town on a weekend. I

remember the first time we went into town with our
five bucks, it was a blow-out. We went in this beer joint
and this feller, his name was Rockwell, we called him
'Roxy'; he had a damn fox on a leash and walked it right
up to the bar. Well, after a while old Stoneman's hound
come out from the back and, of course the fox was
female, so you can imagine what happened! They had to
throw a bucket of beer all over 'em to separate 'em and
Stoneman got all pissed off 'cause they throwed beer
on his dog, and boy the fight was on! I was just about to
eat a cheeseburger and some drunk was beating on my
buddy so I just took the bun off that burger, slathered it
up with as much mustard and ketchup as I could, and–
you know that 'ol 'pie in the face' stuff you used to see
on that Soupy Sales show? I gave him a 'pie in the face,'
but it was a cheeseburger in the face. He was bigger than
me and he just worked me up one end of that bar and
down the other before he threw me out the door. Finally,
the truck came and we all piled in. Once we got back to
the camp they couldn't touch us, we were under federal
protection. They had a crew waiting for us next time
we came to town, but we throwed some ax handles in
the truck that time. Of course all that fighting just got us
ready for the war."

Jolly would drive past that pavilion every day and always thought of his uncle and the part he played in the great adventure of building the park.

Early that Sunday morning he let the hot water tap run for a few minutes until the water was hot enough for the instant coffee that he had spooned into the cup. Since his wife Eva had left him a few years back he had switched to instant purely for practical reasons. Though his nephew called it "retarded chocolate milk," it wasn't that bad. As he stood over the sink sipping his coffee, Jolly looked out over his property through the kitchen window, and his thoughts wandered.

It was early November, and nearly another year had passed. It seemed like last week it was still summer, and he and Floyd Boggess were baling hay. Poor old Floyd; he could see him sitting in the shade eating from a small can of potted meat with his pocketknife talking about his grandkids. Fishing through his tattered wallet for dog-eared, faded school photos of junior high aged kids and passing them to Jolly as he told him about each one. Of course, Jolly knew that each of them were now grown, mature adults, living far away, maybe to come home for Thanksgiving once every five years or so—maybe not. They were among the many who had left, including

Jolly's own daughter Valerie who set out on her own for
Charlotte years ago. Old Floyd either just didn't want to
accept that they were grown and gone, or he was just not
living in the present.

It was last summer Jolly quit going to church
as well. When his wife moved out and went up to
Clarksburg to live with her sister, Jolly continued going to
church. He even mowed the church lawn and trimmed
around the swingset and picnic tables just to be helpful.
For a while it seemed like there was sympathy for him
that his wife had left him; after all there was no infidelity
involved. They had just grown apart, and she wanted
to live somewhere else. Then gradually it seemed many
of the church women decided that for some reason
or another, he was not a good person. He could tell a
shifting of alliances taking place, a new and menacing
outer coldness in their demeanors.

The final straw was when one of them saw him
at the local grocery store and informed him of a new
canned food drive for the church. He smiled and nodded
until she told him that "there's still time for you to buy
some cans and drop them off at the church—to deal
with the guilt, if there is any." With that remark he never
set foot in that church again. What guilt? He decided

they were all crazy. Hell, what did he ever do to them anyway? How people could be so self-righteous and judgmental was beyond him, which reminded him that he had already decided not to let the church women use his farm again this year to make apple butter.

November meant another deer season. When he was younger it used to be the highlight of his year. How many times had he embraced the predawn silence in his deer stand and anxiously awaited the rising sun, as the surreal sounds of crowing roosters and the ragged barking of hounds echoed across the valley? He would pile into the truck with his brothers, son, and nephews, and they would hunt for the whole week of Thanksgiving. It was his favorite week of the year.

He eyed the old Marlin 30-30 with the high-mounted scope resting in the corner of the kitchen. He had set it there just the other day in anticipation, though he no longer really hunted deer; he just shot them. Last year he shot one from his kitchen window. It was so close he didn't need the scope but used the iron sights visible below the high scope mount. The year before he got one from the rocking chair on the porch just at dusk. He often kept the rifle handy for coyotes as well, he had managed to kill three of the elusive predators over the years. Like the garden vegetables he canned each summer, he also canned his venison. He usually killed two or three deer a year. He wasn't greedy; he ate everything he killed. At his age he felt he was too old to walk the ridges and drag deer like he used to when he was young and besides, Taylors had been killing deer for over two hundred years, he recalled.

The biggest problem he saw now with hunting anymore was the damn climate. His best hunting memories included deep snow and frozen ruts. He remembered his grandfather telling him stories about how his father knew of streams up in the mountains where patches of ice lasted all through the summer months in the most shaded recesses and deep hollows. Last year on the opening day of hunting season, it seemed muggy in the mid-fifties with mud and rain instead of ice and snow. Those people who don't believe in global warming must not be deer hunters. He heard that they even had some gators across the mountains down on the southern coast of Virginia now. Climate change or not he would still kill a deer, he was just too old to work for it anymore.

Leaving his coffee cup on the counter he decided to take a walk in the cool morning air. He ran his hand through his thinning hair, the color of yellowed mayonnaise, before twisting his ball cap in place and putting on his blanket-lined barn jacket. He gave a sharp whistle and his old dog Loop, an Australian blue healer, rose from his place near the wood stove and followed Jolly out of the door. The air was just cold enough to make his eyes water a bit, and he put his hands in his pockets as he traipsed across the slightly frozen muddy ground. He walked across the lot, past the barn, and up the gentle rise that led to the high fields and wood line that bordered his property.

The faded stubble fields of autumn greeted him as he reached the top of the hill where the ground flattened out. Moisture from the stubble clung to the cuffs of his green work pants and lace-up leather boots as he gently walked toward the woodline—one of the highest points on the farm. Here and there large limestone outcroppings jutted out of the ground. Much of the surrounding area was riddled with caves and pits of various sizes as the land was honeycombed with caverns and other dark places. The county was a well-known destination for spelunkers and school groups, who studied the caves, and scientists, who studied bats and other underground phenomena. Jolly had been in some of the more easily accessible caves when he was younger but now, he had no desire to repeat the experience. He was sure he knew where every pit and hole existed on his land, but he still walked with care and marked his steps while walking alone.

There was one exceptionally large pit up at the edge of the field that was the suspected culprit for the loss of more than one cow and sheep over the years. It was just beyond what they called Turtle Rock, named for the large limestone outcropping, which resembled a giant turtle somehow, at least that was how it must have looked to the distant ancestor who named it. Over time the pit became known as The Big Hole. Jolly and his brothers tried to rappel down in there once when they were in junior high, but they soon chickened out and never ventured all the way down, if that was possible—it seemed bottomless. It was definitely large enough to swallow up more than a cow.

The creek was down at the moment, but evidence of recent heavy rains was left behind in the form of debris that had been washed down with the rushing waters. A child's muddy kickball, several old rubber tires that he had not seen before, various bottles, and a few plastic bags clung to the edge of the creek bank. In the tree above more plastic bags hung from the lowest-lying branches over the creek indicating a high-water mark. Down the field he noticed a colored foil party balloon that had once held helium and been released into the air long ago swaying in the gentle breeze, its long stringy tail tangled in a tree limb.

Part of the creek was bisected occasionally by strands of barbed wire fencing that had been there since before he could remember. A stone's throw from the barbed wire was the hollow beech tree where he used to hunt bear. He could see the notch he had cut long ago into the tree with a chainsaw. He used to fill the tree with dozens of day-old donuts and vanilla extract and wait. When a bear reached his head or front leg into the notch to get to the donuts, he would become stuck in the notch, and Jolly would shoot him. He got several that way, but he quit bear hunting after Alan's accident.

His son Alan used to hunt with him, and they had a strong bond. It didn't matter if they killed anything or not; it was just good to hunt with him when they could. Alan had been killed over twenty years ago, about the time his niece Lori had been attacked over on 219 when his nephew Snap was just a baby. Alan had been driving a log truck up I-79 when a deer darted across the road.

He instinctively swerved to miss it while trucking uphill trying to pass a slower truck. The load shifted, and Alan's truck angled into the sunken median landing on the driver's side. The State Police called to tell him that Alan was dead at the scene. Though she never came out and said it, Jolly knew that the accident was part of the reason his wife had moved out. She couldn't take his bouts of silence and lack of communication that often seized his moods after that, especially in the evenings.

He used to sit in the kitchen with a cup of coffee and softly strum his old Guild guitar when he was in one of his moods, and she never seemed to understand. She would enter the room, noisily turn on the tap, clank dishes and silverware around, and open and slam cabinet doors as if he wasn't even there. Instead of talking or consoling each other, they drifted apart and then one day she left. Well, perhaps it was for the best. He still loved her, but these days he needed to be alone as well.

Beyond the hollow beech, Jolly found the old fire ring. He kicked at the last remnants of charcoal and thought of how long it had been since he had camped up here. When he was a boy, he used to come up here with a .22 rifle and a bed roll. He would shoot a rabbit, and then build a fire. He remembered holding the rabbit by its hind legs, stepping on its head and pulling until the head tore away from the body. In less than a minute he would have it skinned and cleaned, "pulling off its pajamas," and removing the entrails with his pocketknife. In his pocket he always carried some bailing twine, an old dog chain, and a small hand-forged hook he had found in the barn.

He then built a tripod out of three tree limbs, fastening them together with the baling twine and hung the dog chain and hook down from the tripod. Next he wrapped some twine around the rabbit and hooked it to the chain. After he had built the fire, he would lay the tripod over the fire and set up his camp for the night while the rabbit cooked.

As he looked down at the cold shards of charcoal, partly buried under dried leaves and field debris, he wondered what had happened to the chain and hook. He still had the rifle, though he had given it to Alan when he was twelve. He scraped the fire pit one more time with his boot and walked on.

Twenty feet beyond the fire pit, not far from where he laid out his salt blocks, he saw a glint of bright sunlight on the ground. Upon inspection he saw that it was the sun's reflection on a partially buried piece of amber-colored glass. He knelt and wiggled it out of the dirt and saw it was an old Stroh's bottle. The antiquated label dated it to the late '70s shortly after he got out of the service. He soon found seven more bottles in the vicinity, though he knew more had been consumed. He remembered drinking up here one time with Trick Diehl and some other guys one weekend long ago. They had gotten a couple of cases, had a big bonfire up on the hill, and got out their guitars. He remembered his future wife had stopped by for a while with some of her friends but left before it got too crazy. Every star in the universe seemed to be lit up that night. It had been years since he'd seen Trick. That was not long after his niece Lori was born. He threw the dirty bottle in a long arc back among the trees to rest with all the other buried memories on the hill.

From the high vantage point, he scanned the landscape below. He knew every mountain in the distance and the path that his ancestors had taken into the valley when they first claimed it with tomahawk rights. He knew every curve in that road below, and every spot to fish in every stream for miles in any direction. On a far hillside he could just make out the

family cemetery, where generations of Taylors were laid
to rest, the markers varying from timeworn leaning slabs
of field stone with crude engraving to modern glossy
marble. Ancient locust fence posts, still hard as steel,
surrounded the little graveyard and delineated it from
the rest of the property.

The barn below was visible where it housed
generations of equipment of every kind. The tractor,
hay wagon, baler, forge and the farrier tools, yokes,
harnesses, reins, the cane press, the old wagon, even the
remnants of a carriage, wagon wheels, horseshoes, and
nail kegs, were all safe there amid the silence, darkness,
and dust. In the field across from the barn the hulls of
over half a dozen automobiles sat in a line, each year
sinking a little further into the ground and showing a
little more rust. Nearly every generation was represented
from the '50s onward. One of the cars had been Alan's.
The keys to all of them were in a drawer somewhere in
the house.

The farmhouse itself had been built in the mid-
19th century and gradually improved throughout the
years. The dark green shingles contrasted with the dirty
whiteboards and the two brick chimneys. The stove
pipe and crooked TV antennae jutted out on opposite

ends of the roof, as the large wrap-around porch offered shade from the sun and protection from the rain for God knows how many Taylors over the years. A full quarter of the porch sheltered stacked stove wood. It was a large porch for one man to sit alone comfortably with so many ghosts and reminders of the past hanging about. Jolly found his eyes were still watery, though it was no longer from the cold.

Chapter 3. Missing

It took forty-five minutes for Jolly to get home from the state park. November was a slow time, and Taylors Notch was one of the few state parks that remained open throughout winter due to its proximity to ski country. He left the park grounds and headed back for home, planning on stopping in town on the way. With one hand on the wheel, he rolled along, a cup of warm coffee in his right. He wished it stayed light longer this time of year as he drove to and from work in the dark. Each day he passed the wide spot on the road where his niece Lori had been attacked over twenty years ago not long after her son Snap was born. At least she was still alive, not like the others, including the one who was never found.

Maynard's was the one beer joint in Taylor Meadows, and Jolly felt comfortable there. He'd stop by to have a few beers and sometimes a bite to eat. There was a limited menu, and since he lived alone, Jolly ate there several nights a week. Besides the fact it was on the way home, it was also as much for the company as for the food.

He sat at one of the six booths across from the bar. Joanie left her spot behind to bar to bring him a long neck and swipe the table, while he ordered a cheeseburger and fries with slaw on the side. Four other men he knew were sitting at the bar. He had been coming into that beer joint since he was a teenager, and he reflected on how little it had changed over the years. The off-white-colored walls and slat ceiling, the mounted deer head, the shiny small mouth bass mounted to a plaque, all had been there for years. The stove pipe curled into the far wall just above the ceiling right above an old metal sign imploring the customer to "Drink Ski." Nearby several oval-shaped pine slabs held yellowed, shellacked photographs of rural scenes from somewhere in the county, all were very familiar to him. Lori's rape, the death of his son, his wife leaving, the presence of windmills on the ridges outside of town, the crazy weather patterns—at least this place never changed.

Jolly almost saw his first bar fight here once long ago. A group of musicians were crowded in the corner preparing to play some tunes, and a local drunk kept

turning on the juke box. Maynard's really wasn't set up
for live music, but this family band had stopped in for
some beers on their way to a real gig later that night.
The owner told them it was on the house if they played
a few songs. The fiddler was just ready to kick one off
when the juke box came on. They let the song finish and
when it was apparent that the drunk had a handful of
change for more records, the banjo player walked over
to the juke box. He pulled out his jack knife and sawed
on the electrical cord until it was severed, and exclaimed,
"Fellers, we're fixin' to play some music here." Though
not pleased, the drunk was outnumbered and left before
a fight could ensue. Good memories.

Joanie brought Jolly his supper and another beer.
Though she was always cheerful around Jolly, he sensed
she was sometimes very troubled. He would notice her
behind the bar when she wasn't busy serving drinks, and
he felt she carried an unspoken air of sadness about her.
He had heard that her marriage was not so good and that
she might even be looking for a new place to stay for a
while. Jolly thought she was one of the best-looking fifty-
year-old women he had ever seen. He wasn't ashamed to
think how he would like to just watch her take a shower.
She was heavy-bosomed, large-hipped, and walked as if

she had ridden a lot of horses in her life, which she had. She had baled her share of hay, helped deliver the calves, and could do just about anything around the farm. She married and had kids young. Now her daughters were married and gone, and her mechanic husband had grown distant over the past few years. She had been saving her money in case she might need to make a clean break and head off on her own. Jolly gave her a smile and thanked her as she set down his plate and beer with hands that smelled of cigarettes and bleach. She gave him a wry smile and headed back behind the bar.

After taking his time with his meal he gravitated to the bar where several other men he knew were drinking and looking at the weather channel on the muted television which was set over the bar. Looking past the plastic donation bucket for the local volunteer fire department, Jolly's eyes darted from one liquor bottle to another behind the bar and over to the American flag hanging above the mirror. It was made of heavy cloth and had brass grommets and 48 stars. He knew how many stars there were because he had sat there and counted them many times over the years. Near the door was a corkboard peppered with thumbtacks.

Anyone who wanted to leave a message or advertise a service was welcome to use it for a community bulletin board. A number of business cards were mixed in with handwritten notes or colorful ads printed on a computer advertised everything from veterinary services, tattoos, and manure, to spray bed liners or tinted windows for pickup trucks. Jolly made out the word "missing," on one of the oldest posters tacked to the board. It was virtually covered by the more recent cards and papers. He knew who that missing poster was for, and it was a constant reminder of Lori's rape that same year, 1997.

Three young women had been attacked that year on 219. Lori was the only one they didn't kill. Jolly was surprised that the missing poster for the one girl was still on the bulletin board after all these years, but then Maynard's was not a place that changed much. It seemed surprising that no arrests had ever been made. Jolly couldn't shake the feeling that it had to be somebody local, within proximity of the crimes at least. It could have been anybody passing through, but with three women attacked, it had to be someone from at least in the county.

It also ate at Jolly how this crime had affected his family. Lori was still alive and that was good, but it sure messed her up. Lori was special to him, his oldest niece. Such a sweet girl. Who knew how different a mother she could have been to her son, Snap, if this had not happened? She changed so much after that, turning to drinking and started taking those damn pills to cope with it all. No wonder Snap was so screwed up too. He could be a good kid when he wasn't on drugs himself, but was now a lost cause. After another slow beer Jolly was ready to head on home. As he started the truck, he remembered he had to stop by the little grocery store for some milk, coffee, and beer.

As he reached for his wallet to pay for his groceries in the little store, he struck up a conversation with the cashier. She asked about his wife and then mentioned that his great-nephew Snap had been in earlier buying beer and cigarettes. Though he had known him since he was born, Snap was a loose cannon. It was good to get a heads-up that he was in the area.

Chapter 4. *Two Guitars and a Rifle*

Jolly knew that something was wrong when he pulled up to the house; he could just sense it. He sat in the truck for a moment and then realized that one of the fence posts just opposite the house was knocked backward at a steep angle. He retrieved a flashlight and a small automatic pistol from the glove box and slowly walked the fence line shining the light along the way. He whistled for Loop, and the dog was soon walking with him. "Who was it Loop?" he asked, rubbing the dog's head, as he went on inspecting the fence. One upright and two horizontal boards had been knocked out of whack. Someone had gunned it in reverse too fast trying to exit the farm and had backed into the fence line.

The kitchen door was closed but just barely as he pushed it open with his left boot. After turning on the overhead light he slowly checked out the kitchen. At first glance, everything seemed to be in place. The walking

sticks were behind the door beneath some cobwebs;
the old refrigerator was humming, and the pilot light
was still on at the gas stove. The wood stove was lightly
glowing. He picked up the receiver on the landline and
a dial tone was present. The table looked normal, and
then he looked down at the old, cracked linoleum floor
and followed it over to the corner. His Marlin rifle was
conspicuously missing, as he had expected. So, they got
that.

He methodically walked through the rest of the
house room by room, turning on all the lights one at a
time. His bedroom looked undisturbed except for the one
open drawer, the top drawer of his dresser. He opened
it further and saw that several of his personal items
were missing: an old pocket watch that had been his
grandfather's, several pocketknives that had sentimental
value, and an odd assortment of coins and currency
from various foreign countries that he had acquired over
the years. His gun safe, which he had bolted to the floor
and wall studs, was still intact but had been beaten. He
fumbled for his keys and unlocked the safe. The door
was damaged, but his other guns were still in place. In
the hallway, he noticed that the closet door was ajar.

A pair of his best Carhart coveralls were gone, along

with all the winter coats and boots. Though he had been
robbed the house did not have a ransacked look. One of
the pictures on the wall was crooked as if someone had
passed through the hallway in a hurry and their shoulder
brushed the protruding frame.

Lastly, he inspected the back room. An independent
observer would have noticed that this room seemed to
be lost in time. The clock on the wall was an hour behind
since no one ever adjusted it for daylight saving time;
the curtains were never drawn, and the room was kept
perpetually dark. The orange-tinted pattern wallpaper
and tan carpet gave the room a strange glow, especially
when the evening sun seeped in between the edges of
the curtains. An old stereo record player and a stack of
records sat on top of a large wooden television console,
all of which were covered with dust. Jolly couldn't
remember the last time the stereo or the television
had been turned on. Several framed glossy family
photographs hung on the wall beside a coat rack covered
in jackets and antiquated hats.

Jolly switched on the light and immediately
noticed that his two guitars were missing from their
normal perch on the quilt-covered loveseat. Both the
old Silvertone that had been in his family since he was

a kid and a jumbo Guild that he had bought in his early twenties, were gone–the cases too–which were always stored against the wall in the corner. It was kind of funny; they only took things that meant something to him. Why didn't they take all the old junk in this room and leave the guitars? It was almost as if this operation was more like a surgical removal than an actual robbery.

He then checked the rest of the rooms in the house. He slowly walked up the narrow stairwell and heard his work boots slightly echo on the hardwood no matter how quiet he tried to be. From what he could tell it didn't look like they had reached the upstairs. He searched each room and the closets. Then he remembered something and checked in the back closet of one of the guest rooms. It was still there, deep in the corner of the closet behind a rack of old clothes and coats: his grandfather's Springfield .45-70 trapdoor rifle. It was nothing too special; so many of them were made that they were a dime a dozen at one time. but this one had been his grandfather's. It had been kept in that closet for as long as Jolly could remember. He left it where it was and moved on.

Jolly turned off the light as he left the room, returned downstairs to the kitchen, opened the fridge, and took out a beer. He pulled a chair away from the table and leaned back taking a long pull on the bottle. Suddenly he realized that his hands were shaking. He was pissed off like he hadn't been in years. It could have been worse, but his rifle, his coveralls, his guitars, his pocketknives . . . he sure as hell didn't deserve being treated like this. He stared at the wall and instinctively reached into his left-hand shirt pocket and pulled out a pack of cigarettes, shook one out into his lips and set the pack down on the table beside his pistol and flashlight. He snapped the lighter, inhaled deeply and blew the smoke across the room toward the empty corner where his rifle had been. Three beers and six cigarettes later, he figured out what he was going to do.

Chapter 5. 1972 GTO

Jolly assumed whoever they were would probably be back. He had better take some new precautions. One thing about thieves is that they are cowards, and any resistance will most likely run them off. After some searching, he found the correct drawer and the right key he was looking for, along with his headlamp. With his headlamp fastened under the bill of his ball cap, a beer in his hand, and his pistol in his back pocket he walked out the door and into the yard. The row of old cars had sat there for years on end, and he never questioned the tradition of leaving unused vehicles on the property. He stopped at what had been Alan's favorite, a 1972 Pontiac GTO. Alan had fixed it up and used to cruise around the county in it with his girlfriend on sunny Saturdays, and he even used to take it to the State Folk Festival in Glenville for the old car show for a couple of years. Now, it had rested here at the edge of the field since

Alan's death, and Jolly was about to bring it back into
use.

The trunk opened, and Jolly felt around inside it
using his flashlight to see how airtight it was. Jolly was
glad to see that it was dry. After lining the trunk with a
poly tarp and a wool blanket, he laid the contents of the
damaged gun safe onto his bed and then made several
trips carrying the guns from the bed to the trunk of the
GTO. He had a .22 rifle, an old model 12 Winchester
12-gauge pump shotgun, a single-shot 12-gauge shotgun,
a .410 shotgun, and several pistols. He kept the pump
and a Ruger Blackhawk .357 Magnum revolver, the other
firearms, and the ammunition, he stored in the trunk of
the car then attached the key to his keychain.

The next morning, he fried some eggs and bologna
and coffee for breakfast. As he finished the coffee, he
stared out of the kitchen window at the damaged fence.
It was easier to tell what had happened in the daylight.
From the tire treads it looked like a large-framed pickup.
He would have liked to have taken a picture of the tire
treads, but he didn't own a camera. Over by the fence
he found a shard of red plastic which, apparently, had
broken out of a taillight. He pocketed the red plastic and
walked over to the GTO, opened the trunk, and inspected

his ammunition. He found a partial box of 12-gauge number 4's and a box of .357's. He also found an extra magazine for the small automatic which served as his glovebox gun. He decided to keep the shotgun and the revolver behind the seat of his truck and then move them into the house when he was home. They wouldn't catch him off guard again.

The whole time since he discovered the theft it never occurred to him to call the sheriff. He had a pretty good idea who robbed him, and he already had a plan to try and get his stuff back. The Taylors had lived on this land long enough to have been robbed before, and they knew how to deal with it.

Chapter 6. Road Trip

The Saturday after the theft Jolly rose early and was on the road just at sunup. He stopped off at the little diner in Taylor Meadows for a sausage biscuit and coffee to go and then continued south on 219. He drove first to Lewisburg and stopped in all the pawn shops he could find inquiring about his rifle and his guitars. He also asked about pocketknives and the pocket watch. He left each store his phone number and visited a large indoor flea market whose ranks would swell into the parking lot when summer hit. All day Jolly drove back up 219 toward Elkins and then onto Route 33 all the way to Weston. He stopped in every pawn, gun, and junk shop he could find and anywhere else that his stolen merchandise could show up. He was certain that his efforts would be rewarded before too long. Of course, he could be completely wrong, but he figured action was better than inaction. Besides, the trip allowed him to choose between four different Walmarts should he decide to get some supplies. He decided to make a large loop and head home through Webster County, exiting the interstate at Flatwoods and then cutting through the Back Fork of Elk, over Point Mountain and then to Valley Head. He had enough acquaintances along that route to make inquiries about his stolen goods.

It was late when he got home, and he was completely worn out from over ten hours of hard driving, most of it on curvy two-lane roads. He also put the word out to all his trusted friends to be on the lookout for his rifle and guitars, and to let him know if they heard any news about his great-nephew. The next day he called Lori who now lived in Charleston. He waited until the early afternoon, so he could catch her after church. She sounded like she was doing well, and she was excited to hear from her uncle. He asked about everyone in her family in turn, eventually getting to her son Snap.

"So how is Snap doing?" Jolly asked.

"Well, he's been doing pretty good." He could hear a rustle as Loir shifted the phone. "You know he doesn't live here anymore. He moved back in after the first time he moved out, but it didn't last. I mean at his age, he really needs to be out on his own. But he did stop by this past week, on Thursday I believe. You know, he's always liked playing guitar ..."

"I know, I taught him." Jolly chuckled, his voice sounding light and happy.

"That's right, you did. Well, he showed up last Thursday with three new guitars, well, new to him. Said he was in a new band, and he wanted me to keep them for him for a little while."

"Three guitars? Are you sure it was three?"

"I'm pretty sure he came in with three guitar cases. I had him put them back in his old room until he needed them."

"Well, that's great, so he's been playin' in a band? Has he been workin' anywhere else?"

"Well, was working for a carnival, but he has trouble passing those drug tests; you know I did too for a while."

"Are you doing better now, honey?" Jolly said with genuine concern.

"Oh yes, glory to God, I'm doing much better. I got hired on at Kroger's, and things have been going as well as can be expected."

"I am glad to hear it. Say, you wouldn't have Snap's phone number would ya? I'd love to get together and play some guitar with him someday, maybe even have him out to the farm."

That night, Jolly went through a few photo albums until he found the pictures he wanted and readied himself for another road trip. He rummaged through a desk drawer until he found two envelopes and a pad of paper. He wrote a short letter and placed it in one envelope along with some cash, and in the second envelope, he placed only the photos.

He had some vacation time coming and called his boss to tell him that he'd be taking two weeks off to take care of some family business. It was the slow season, so his boss told him to have a good week. Jolly packed an overnight bag, just in case, and readied himself for bed. He had another long drive tomorrow.

Jolly left home once again at the break of day, stopped off at the diner for two sausage biscuits, filled up his thermos, and hit the road, this time for Charleston. He was sick of 219, so he cut across the county along a series of back roads. He drove north and then cut across the country along a series of back roads. There was a skim of snow on the high ridges as he drove along the old graveled, seasonal road, but the weather was still warm enough for the road to be open. After passing Big Ditch Lake he wound his way to Birch River, and eventually over to the interstate an hour north of Charleston. It took him nearly four hours to reach his destination, but he made it. He had called ahead from a phone at a gas station and told Lori he would be in Charleston and would like to stop in; she said she would be off work at three and then would meet him at the house. She told him where to find the key and told him to make himself at home.

Jolly arched his back and shook off the road as he found the key in the potted plant on the landing and unlocked the door. He wiped his feet on the mat and then entered the house. He always felt funny being in another person's home while they were away—too bad more people didn't feel that way, maybe he'd still have his shit. He had no intention of waiting for his niece to get home before he got what he came for.

He found three guitar cases in the side bedroom down the hall from the kitchen and across from the tiny bathroom. He laid each out on the twin bed in the small room. After opening each case, he found his Silvertone, his Guild, and, of all things, the third guitar—which turned out to be his Marlin rifle. "Well, that's family for you," he said as he worked the action of the rifle and found that it was still loaded, and that was just fine as far as he was concerned. After casing up the instruments he loaded them into his truck with the guitars on the passenger seat and the rifle behind the seat. Before he left, he placed the envelopes, one addressed to "Lori" and the other addressed to "Snap," on the kitchen counter. The envelope addressed to Snap contained old photos of Uncle Jolly playing the two stolen guitars and one of him and Snap playing them together when Snap was a young boy.

Chapter 7. O What a Blessed Reunion

That evening as Jolly passed through Taylor Meadows and was nearly home, he stopped off at the home of an old friend and dropped off the two guitars. He asked if the man could just keep them for him for a while, and he was certainly welcome to play them if he wanted to. The friend agreed with no questions asked, and Jolly headed home.

Later that night Lori called. She was crying and upset. She came home from work and read Jolly's note and she understood what was going on. Snap came in a few hours later and "went a little nuts" when he found out what had happened. He tore up the photos and punched a hole in the drywall. Jolly apologized for causing her so much distress and said that he figured something like that might happen, that was why he had put some cash in the envelope. The bottom line was that Snap was now on a tear and she had no idea where he was. And no, he hadn't hurt her, but she was awful afraid of what he might do.

Two days later Jolly received another phone call from one of his buddies. Snap had been through Taylor Meadows, stopped at the store, and was shacked up outside of town with a woman he often stayed with when he was up this way. Jolly wrote down the directions and decided to pay Snap a little visit the next day. Jolly figured the best way to catch Snap off guard was to show up early in the morning. He figured Snap was tweaking and he may not even be in bed yet, or he would be crashed out. Either way Jolly would have the advantage.

It was dawn when Jolly left the farm for his recent morning routine of a sausage biscuit and coffee to go at the diner. With the .357 on the passenger seat, he drove down the forest-lined country back roads until he came to a gravel road that crossed a creek and up over another ridge to a rutted-out lane that led to a single-wide trailer. A lone electrical pole stood guard in the small clearing near the road where the trailer's foundation had been laid. He gently kicked aside some dirty plastic toys in the yard and walked over to the black pickup parked catty-wumpus in the yard next to a beat-up purple Dodge Charger. The first thing he noticed was that the left rear taillight was damaged. He reached into his pocket and matched the piece he had found in his driveway with the broken red plastic on the taillight. He then saw that something looked awfully funny about the paint job on this truck, it was black, but a weird black. He had never seen anything quite like it. It felt coarse and rubbery to the touch. After checking the cab for his pocketknives, he walked up to the trailer.

The pounding on the door at 6:30 am must have sounded like thunder to those inside. He heard a woman shout something, some kids squeal, and then finally thumping footsteps. The door opened and Jolly's fist smashed straight into Snap's jaw knocking him backward into an ocean of child's toys and household trash. He heard a woman scream and the bedroom door slam as he dragged his great-nephew down the steps of the homemade porch and out into the yard. It was then he got his first real look at the kid he hadn't seen since last Christmas, and he looked like a real piece of shit.

As he lay there on the cold November ground rubbing his jaw, Jolly cold see that Snap wasn't doing too well for himself. Both ears were mutilated with nickel-sized rubber gauges, the tattoos covered his neck and most of his arms. Jolly had nothing against people with tattoos or piercings, but this sure didn't look healthy. The stringy dark hair looked like it hadn't been washed in a week or so, and his clothes were pretty much filthy. But it was his eyes that really got to Jolly; they were the eyes of a very sad, desperate human being who probably wished he'd made some better life choices. Jolly didn't see the anger that Lori described in those eyes; he only saw fear, sadness, and to Jolly's relief, perhaps some regret. He was about to find out if it was regret for stealing from his great-uncle or regret for getting caught.

Jolly towered over Snap as he used his elbow to shift to a sitting position. He made no attempt to lash out at Jolly and instead, just sat there. Then Jolly started in on him.

"What the hell's wrong with you, goddammit? I've been nothing but nice to you and your mama your whole life and you break in my house and steal from me? Did you think I wouldn't figure out who done it? Are you that goddamn stupid?" Jolly noticed faces at the dirty window of the trailer but ignored them. "And knockin' a hole in your mama's wall. I ought'a knock a hole in your head! If you ever lay a hand on that woman, I will hit you so goddamn hard your grandchildren will be born screamin'!"

"I'm sorry uncle Jolly." The voice was flat and weak sounding. "I know'd it was wrong, I just can't help it. I needed money."

"Did you ever think to just ask? Or, better yet, get a job? Robbin' your own blood? I outta beat the livin' shit ought'a you! You need to get your act together Snap. The next guy you steal from might not be so understanding. And where's my pocketknives and Carhart's you stole?"

"They're gone. I sold 'em."

"Sold 'em to who?"

"Nobody you'd know."

"Well," Jolly held out his hand, "get yer ass up." He helped Snap up and looked him square in the eye. "Now don't you ever steal from me again. In fact, I don't want to ever see you around my place again. I'll call you if I want to see you again. And get off that damn dope and try to get a hold of yourself, you're too young to piss your life away on that shit."

Snap, shivering in his bare feet and t-shirt in the cold November air, lowered his head in humiliation, "I'll try, Uncle Jolly, I am sorry. I'll…I'll stay away," he said as he nodded and accepted the offered cigarette from his uncle. They both lit up and Jolly took a step back and pointed at Snap with his cigarette.

"Okay. Now I'm gonna call your mama once in a while and check in on you. And don't ever think that I can't find you. I've lived in this county a hell of a lot longer than you have." Snap nodded his head and kept it bowed. Jolly nodded and turned to leave, then turned for one last question. "By the way, what's that black shit all over your truck? It don't look like paint."

"It's Flex Seal."

"It's what?"

"Flex Seal."

"You painted your truck with Flex Seal? What the hell for?"

"It's supposed to make it stealth." He bobbed his head back a few degrees and looked to the sky for imaginary airplanes. "You know, like those stealth fighters that can resist radar? The cop's laser beams just bounce off it so they can't catch you speedin'." With that Jolly just shook his head, got in his truck, and left.

Chapter 8. Blood in the High Field

With Thanksgiving and deer season a week and a
half away, Jolly decided that it was time to get some meat
for the larder. He set the Ruger .357 on the passenger
seat of his truck next to a long black flashlight and
drove up onto the high fields above the house just after
sundown. He had several salt blocks set on fence posts
up in that field, and he could tell from all the droppings
and other signs that the deer had been patronizing them
well. The blocks themselves were partially chewed and
licked down by at least a good third from their original
size, and that could only mean one thing. The white salt
lit up brightly in the headlights of the truck as he wheeled
around and positioned it about twenty-five yards from,
and parallel to, the fence post with the passenger side
window facing the salt blocks. He then moved to the
passenger seat, turned off the lights, cracked open a beer
and patiently waited. The final dim glow on the rim of

the western horizon gave way to total darkness and the stars began to appear overhead like magic Christmas lights. The silence in the field was deafening, and Jolly found it totally relaxing.

It was cold in the cab with the window rolled down, and he could see his breath, but he was bundled up in the new set of coveralls he'd bought to replace the ones that were stolen. He also brought along a thermos of hot coffee and a bologna sandwich; in a way, this was sort of like an interactive drive-in movie of sorts, where you get to shoot the screen.

The slow nature of being in a hunting stand always gave him a chance to think and his mind wandered as he waited for a deer to show up at the salt block. He knew his daughter, Valerie, would be up from Charlotte to spend the Thanksgiving weekend with him and he was anxious to see her. She was bringing her new boyfriend and, from what she told him over the phone, he sounded like a pretty nice guy. He didn't have his hopes up though; it would be good to see her. She was having big problems finding a decent man after her divorce five years ago.

The wild card was if his wife Eva would show up. He figured she would since Val would be there, in fact he sincerely hoped she would. It had been a long time since he'd seen her, and maybe such a visit would bring them a little closer together again. He had to remind himself to call Valerie soon to figure out just how much to cook and what they wanted to eat. He hoped her new boyfriend wasn't a vegan-tarian or one of those people who didn't eat meat. I guess he could just live on instant coffee for a few days if that was the case, Jolly thought as he finished his beer. He quietly set the can down beneath the passenger seat.

Before long he sensed movement in the field and knew that some deer had ambled up to the salt block. Holding the flashlight in his left hand, he carefully cocked the Ruger .357 Magnum and pointed it out of the window. He had never shot a deer with a revolver before and he wanted to try it; he knew he was a good enough shot. He switched on the flashlight. Instantly five does stood transfixed and frozen in the bright beam, their shining eyes seeming as big as baseballs as they reflected the harsh light back toward Jolly's pistol. Bracing his right forearm against the side of the open window, he aimed a moment then dropped the one nearest to the truck. The other four busted out through the timber as their late companion spun around in a semi-circle and dropped, her hind leg kicking for a moment before ceasing all movement.

Jolly had a cigarette and waited a good while before exiting the truck just in case some snooper suspected what he was up to and called it in. It took him less than ten minutes to have the deer gutted and thrown into the bed of the truck. Then it was down to the barn to hang for the night. He would skin it tomorrow and begin to process the meat for canning after cutting himself a few steaks and tenderloin. The hide he would dispose of like all the others he'd poached. He'd throw it down The Big Hole in the field near Turtle Rock.

Chapter 9. Thanksgiving

Jolly drank his second nervous cup of coffee standing at the kitchen sink looking out of the window as he waited for his daughter and her boyfriend to arrive. It was just past six in the evening, the night before Thanksgiving, and he expected them to be there soon. His estranged wife Eva was supposed to be there by mid-morning tomorrow. He had lived alone so long now that he wasn't really sure how he felt about a house full of visitors even if it was his own family. He had the cup to his lips finishing the last sip when he saw headlights heading up the lane from the hard road.

He leaned on a porch rail then brightened and smiled as they pulled in. He dressed for the occasion as he always did: his blue and gray patterned flannel shirt open at the top revealing the top of his V-neck white t-shirt. His green work pants, well used but clean, and a worn brown leather work belt on which hung the snap sheath for his Schrade lock-blade. Wearing slippers, his lace-up leather work boots were neatly lined up in the hallway near the closet. He greeted them as they exited the large Ford Expedition and started unloading the luggage.

"I'd help ya but I'm in my house slippers!" Jolly yelled as Valerie and the man began a slow, road-weary, walk up to the house with overnight bags on their shoulders. He instinctively took her bag as she stepped up onto the porch, and she gave him a big hug and a kiss. He held her for several seconds with his cheek to hers, his little girl, though not so little anymore. "It's so good to see you honey. How's my baby girl?"

"I'm good daddy. You smell so good. You still use that blue aftershave?"

"Oh, yea, I remember how much you liked it when you was little," he chuckled. "Well, who's your friend here?" He said, while shaking hands with the thin man in the wire-rimmed glasses and neat beard.

"This is Jackson; Jackson, this is my dad, Jolly."

"Nice to meet you, Jolly."

"Good to know you, come on in."

After they had taken their bags upstairs and Valerie had shown Jackson around the house, she introduced him to old Loop, and then they sat down together at the kitchen table. Valerie had just gone out to the car and returned with two plastic grocery bags holding them one stacked upon the other. She set them on the table for Jolly to inspect. "We brought some drinks. There's hard cider, and this is a great craft beer we brought special from Charlotte; I don't think you can get it here." Jolly checked out a bottle of each, and he chose a cider. "That looks different. Are you all hungry? I can whip up some supper pretty quick."

"We haven't eaten for a while, what do you have?"

"Well, the whole fridge is full of turkey and stuff for tomorrow, but I can fry y'all up some fresh venison steaks and some taters and onions if you'd like."

Jackson looked a bit uncertain. "Do you mean, like, deer meat?"

"You bet, fresh too." Then Valerie chimed in, "That would be super, Daddy. Jackson, you should really try it; believe me you'll love it." Then she noticed Jackson staring at the scoped rifle in the corner. She gave Jolly a look with her eyes and nodded her head at the rifle. Jolly looked at both of them, took the hint, and without a word moved it into the bedroom.

Jolly nursed his cider as he got down the cast iron

skillet and set it on the back burner of the gas stove. After cutting strips of venison and rolling them in flour, he proceeded to fry them in butter until they were crispy on the outside and not too soft to the touch. While the venison lightly crackled on the stove, he produced three large potatoes and an onion. After peeling the potatoes and chopping the onion, he took down another cast iron skillet larger than the first one. He then set it on the largest burner and dumped in the potatoes and onion. He reached up into the cabinet near the sink and grabbed a quart mason jar of thick off-white liquid and poured some into the skillet with the potatoes and onions. This got Jackson's attention.

"What's that stuff?"

"Bear grease, I call it mountain butter."

"You kill bears?"

"Used to, but now I get this from a buddy of mine; best grease you'll ever cook with."

He turned the venison strips with a fork until they were perfect and set them aside on a dinner plate. The potatoes and onions were turned and mixed periodically with a large metal spatula until the potatoes were golden brown and the onions were translucent and slightly caramelized. Some salt and pepper, and they were ready.

"All set. I haven't cooked a meal that big in a long time. I sure love cookin', wish I could do it more. It's hard cookin' for just one."

The supper was an amazing success; Jackson said it was one of the best meals he'd ever had. After supper, with the dishes in the sink, they sat around the table and got caught up. Valerie noticed windmills on the ridges on the way up. "How long have they been there?"

"A good while, several years at least. They really bothered me at first, but I got to where I don't even notice 'em anymore."

Jackson, holding his smart phone, "So I'm trying to get this Quiet Zone thing through my head. You just don't have cell service here? I mean, how do you deal with it?"

"Easy, I just don't give a shit. You can't miss something you never had."

"Okay...I guess it will be like camping or something while we're here."

"Oh, Jackson" Valerie chimed in, "it's not that bad; you'll get used to it. Besides, you can live without your phone for a couple of days."

Jolly changed the subject. "Want some coffee?"

"Sure, that would be great. We haven't had any since the Starbucks in Lewisburg."

"Jackson loves him some Starbucks!" Valerie smiled.
Jolly smiled as he got out three cups and turned on
the hot water tap. "All right then, three Starbucks coming
up." Jackson's eyes betrayed his disbelief as he watched
Jolly spoon instant coffee into the cups and then fill each
cup with steaming tap water. "You want milk in your
coffee Jackson, or do you take it black?" Jolly asked as he
handed the guest the first cup. Jackson decided to try it
straight. After the coffee Jolly asked to try one of the craft
beers. "That's pretty good stuff. Almost as good as that
Ying-ling I been drinkin' lately. I got some if you want to
try it, you don't need to ask, just grab one in the fridge
if you want one. By the way, what do you do for a livin'
Jackson?"

Jackson adjusted his glasses, "I'm a tax attorney."

"The two things I hate the most: taxes and
attorneys. Oh well, you can't be all that bad," Jolly
winked, "you sure know a good cup of coffee when you
see it." Valerie laughed putting her hand on Jackson's
shoulder, letting him know that her dad really wasn't
just some redneck asshole who likes to pick on city boys.
Jackson caught the vibe and gave an uncertain smile;
they sat up together until all the beer and cider were
gone.

Chapter 10. Black Friday

Jolly was up early on Thanksgiving morning and had breakfast ready by the time Valerie and Jackson came downstairs. The kitchen table was set, and there were plenty of eggs over easy, fried potatoes, scratch biscuits, and Jolly's favorite, bacon. He loved cooking the bacon on a cookie sheet in the oven. He always kept parchment paper around just in case. He wouldn't do it just for himself, so this was special.

He missed cooking those big family breakfasts on weekends when his kids were little. Valerie could make biscuits before she could read, and Alan liked learning how to flip the eggs. Eva could cook fine, but she knew how much Jolly enjoyed cooking for everyone on the weekends and never interfered. After breakfast, Valerie helped him with the dishes, and they took stock of what they had to cook for Thanksgiving. He had the turkey and all the usual side dishes for Valerie to prepare, Eva would help when she arrived, and they could catch up while cooking the big meal.

All the cooking took Jolly's mind off what always bothered him about any holiday, the fact that Alan was gone. All those years and it still hurt. He knew he'd never get over it; he just had to deal with it. The passing of time took away some of the sting, but the hurt was always there in his gut, and the memory was deep in the back of his mind. It made having Valerie home more meaningful.

Eva arrived along with her widowed sister, and the three women immediately took over the kitchen without fanfare. Valerie had started the turkey and prepped the rest of the food, so that was a bonus for Jolly. He didn't have to talk to Eva right away. They seldom talked on the phone, and he never quite knew what she was thinking anymore.

While the women prepared the meal, Jolly and Jackson sat out on the porch drinking Jolly's beer. As it had the last few years, the weather turned, and there was a heat wave, 42 degrees on Thanksgiving Day. He sure was glad he'd gotten his deer when he did; he wouldn't shoot one in weather this warm. He'd take frozen ruts over mud any day.

The meal was served around two in the afternoon,

and it was very good. Loop moved from his normal spot in front of the wood stove and nuzzled against Jolly's leg hoping for a handout, of which he got several. Eva and Jackson seemed to get along well enough, and no one mentioned Alan being gone. It was no longer necessary to discuss it. It just was, and that was it. Still, his absence left a light shadow over the room that couldn't be talked away anyway, so better to let it rest.

That evening, after the dishes were done, they all sat and talked in a slow, often lapsing conversation but really had nothing too important to say to each other. Jolly and Eva were cordial, and anyone could see that they were glad to be together again, though maybe it was because they both knew that in a day or so they would be apart..

The women left the next morning for Black Friday shopping in Lewisburg, even though Jolly suggested they hit the Black Friday sales in Taylor Meadows instead. That left Jolly and Jackson alone for a day. The first thing Jackson did was show Jolly how to make a real cup of coffee. Jolly watched as Jackson mixed instant coffee, hot water, brown sugar, and evaporated milk from a tin he found in the cupboard. He stirred it briskly and then handed a cup to Jolly.

"Damn, that's pretty good."

"You like it?"

"Sure do."

After a second cup, Jolly had an idea. He left the kitchen and returned with a pair of rubber mud boots. "Here buddy, put these on." Jolly led him out to the barn, opened the side door and they went inside. "I got something in here you might like to try. Ever had any moonshine?" Jolly reached up on a shelf that held several different containers: a can of WD-40, pints of motor oil, a grease gun, sleeves of axle grease, and a half-empty quart jar of clear liquid with some kind of fruit floating in it.

"What is that in the jar?" Jackson asked as Jolly unscrewed the metal ring and removed the rim with his thumbnail. "Pawpaw, have a shot." Jackson took an exploratory sip and then took another.

"Man, that's some good shit."

Jolly chuckled, "It is, ain't it?"

Then it began to rain, and Jolly got another idea. He opened the big double barn doors so they could get some more light in the building and told Jackson he'd be right back. A few minutes later he returned with a paper grocery sack and a long stocked rifle. "Here, give me a hand," he said passing the bag off to Jackson who set it on the seat of the tractor parked just inside the door.

"What's all this Jolly?"

"Well, since it's raining and we can't really do much of nothin' on a day like this, I thought we 'mise well be comfortable and enjoy ourselves. So, I brought us some leftovers from dinner, and this old rifle to shoot. Hell, its better'n watching television."

Jackson reached into the bag and pulled out several bottles of beer, two boxes of long brass cartridges for the trapdoor, a zip lock bag of leftover turkey of both white and dark meat, and four dinner rolls. "Hep yerself, there Jackson. Wait a second, I forgot something." Jolly walked out in the rain to his truck and returned with the earmuffs he kept around for his chainsaw. He never used them himself, but his boss encouraged him to have them handy in case of a spot safety inspection by state officials. "Here, put these on and I'll show you how to load this."

Jolly demonstrated how to load the rifle. He pulled back the hammer to half cock, flipped up the trap door which opened the breech, slid a shell into the chamber, slammed the trap door back into place, cocked the hammer, put the gun to his shoulder, and fired it off. The recoil was substantial. "Now those are smokeless factory loads, but it was originally a black powder cartridge. And this is the gun the calvary had when Custer got his Yankee ass killed at Little Big Horn."

They spent the rest of the day drinking shine, eating leftover turkey with their fingers, wiping their hands on their britches, spitting in the mud, nursing beers, and shooting dirt clods in the field outside the barn with the old .45-70 Springfield. The errant bullets would often hit one of the limestone outcroppings as evidenced by a brilliant flash of white light as the heavy lead slug struck the rock, the power and force of the impact turning the lead into pure energy. Jackson forgot all about the lack of cell service and didn't even ask Jolly to stand fifteen feet away from the entrance of his barn to smoke the occasional cigarette.

When the women returned both men were in the kitchen mixing brown sugar, evaporated milk, and bourbon with instant coffee. The kitchen table was covered with empty beer bottles, a semi-full ashtray, the last of the turkey carcass, a long-barreled dirty rifle, and scattered shell casings. Their faces were beat red and their movements were highly animated. Jackson was wearing a ball cap that Jolly had given him, and both of

their voices were very loud and happy. "Valerie, did you
know Jackson's a damn gourmet coffee maker? Best cup
a coffee I ever had!"

"Are you sure that was all you've been drinking,
Daddy?" laughed Valerie as she gave her dad and
Jackson each a hug in turn. The ladies were amused
and even Eva had to laugh as she realized that this
Thanksgiving had turned out to be the best, least
melancholic holiday they had had in years, and that
Jackson had forgotten that there was "nothing to do" in
the Quiet Zone.

Chapter 11. Bar-Stool Grapevine

It was a tradition at Maynard's to host a customer appreciation buffet during the week of Christmas. Customers had to pay for their drinks, but all the food was on the house. The small gravel lot was full of trucks mostly as Jolly pulled in just after dark. A wreath hung on the outside of the door, and he was greeted by a strand of twinkling lights attached to the inside door frame as he walked inside. The comfortable smell of homemade food combined with the hum of conversation and soft country music from the sound system made him feel welcome, and he immediately relaxed as he slid into a spot at the bar, his normal booth already taken by the larger-than-usual holiday crowd.

He caught Joanie's eye at the other end of the bar and motioned for a beer. She answered with a wink and soon brought him a cold long neck. As he sipped his first beer of the evening, his eyes naturally darted around

the room from the homemade decorations to the silent
television behind the bar, to the crowd at the small buffet
set up on two folding tables along the far wall.

"Be sure to get you some, Jolly, we got plenty,"
Joanie said as she brought him another beer without his
asking. He looked up at her and smiled and couldn't help
noticing that she had on more makeup than usual and a
bare ring finger.

"You're looking good tonight darlin'. If I was just a
little younger, I'd be chasin' you all over."

She gave a mischievous chuckle and answered,
"And I just might let ya catch me." She looked deep into
his eyes for a moment and gave his hand a little squeeze
before heading down to another customer.

After a hearty plate of roast turkey, mashed
potatoes and gravy, corn pudding, green beans, a few
slices of ham, and three deviled eggs, Jolly was too full
for dessert. After placing his dirty plate and silverware
in the big plastic tub in the corner he resumed his seat
at the bar. The place had begun to thin out and was now
full of mostly regulars who sipped beer and made quiet
conversation. Joanie sat her elbows on the bar across
from Jolly and leaned in a bit, her cleavage seemingly on
display just for him. He saw how she noticed his eyes

run from her breasts to her eyes and she smiled as if to say, "I know what you're thinkin'." She had a sexy look with just enough sass to turn him on. Jolly thought that this was fun, but a little uncomfortable at the moment.

"Need anything, Jolly?"

"I could sure use a cup of coffee, if you got any made."

"Sure, I got coffee. It's a little old. I can make a fresh pot."

"Whatever you got's fine with me."

She walked over to the coffee maker at the other end of the bar and returned with a steaming cup and gently placed it in front of him. As Jolly took a sip, Joanie was at her purse taking out a cigarette. Jolly reached for his pack in his shirt pocket and got one for himself which Joanie lit up with her lighter. They slowly looked at each other in a moment of awkward silence. As Jolly reached for the ash tray he wondered where this might be going. He was certainly attracted to this younger woman, but he also knew she was married. She also seemed sort of desperate, which gave him pause. Part of him sure wanted to take her home, but at the same time he considered her a friend and he didn't want to take advantage of her. Each instinctively knew the other was lonely, and Jolly could feel the tension rising, whether it was a good thing or not yet, he could not say.

"You been doin' all right honey?" He said as he took a slow drag and just patiently waited for her answer. His gentle eyes looked into hers to let her know he was a friend who genuinely cared for her. She averted her eyes for a moment, looking off in either direction while putting her cigarette to her lips and then rubbing an eyebrow with the palm of her cigarette hand.

"Oh, fine. I've been doing just fine." She said with a voice that even she didn't believe.

"How's Jerry?"

"Oh, Jerry's— Jerry. Like he always is." She said slowly blowing smoke sideways.

"Well, I see you're not wearing your ring tonight. Is that, uh, on purpose?"

"Yeah, it's on purpose. Thanks for noticing. I feel like I ain't been noticed in a while."

"Well, you look real nice tonight."

"Thanks, Jolly, you're a sweetheart. And I was serious a while back, I really might let ya catch me."

"Well, besides the fact that you're a damn good-lookin' woman, I worry about you sometimes. I think you're a good person and I hate to see you looking troubled."

"Thanks, Jolly, I appreciate that." She rubbed the side of his face for a moment. "I just love you. If I ever leave Jerry, or he ever leaves me, I just may have to come see you some night." He smiled over his cup as he finished his coffee, his ballcap pushed back on his head a bit. Then her expression changed as she seemed to recall something important. "By the way, I meant to tell you, Jerry told me that Clayton Wheeler was in the garage the other day and told Jerry that Trick Deihl's out of jail."

Jolly's eyebrows raised a bit at the news. "Did he say how long he'd been out?"

"Yeah, he told Jerry that he'd gotten out a few weeks ago, and he was trying to get settled back down here somewhere. Clayton had seen him at the thrift store; Trick asked him for a ride to Log Town Road."

"Not Old Log Town Road?"

"No, I'm pretty sure he said Log Town Road. Why did you think Old Log Town Road"

"Old Log Town's where he used to live years ago. I was just wonderin' if he was heading back to that old place. His family still owns some property back there. If he's living back there, he'd be livin' pretty rough. I doubt they even have power hooked up out there anymore."

"I was out there once on a trail ride with some

friends. We were near that area, but I don't remember seeing any houses."

"Used to be a trailer out there but God knows what it looks like now. Probably in shambles. I wonder if he was down around here before Thanksgiving, or if he just got here?" For some reason, Jolly couldn't help feeling a premonition that the trouble he had with Snap was somehow related to Trick. Trick had always been a friend; they had grown up together. He used to be just a regular 'ol good guy until he got on drugs. Nowadays, Jolly considered him an old acquaintance more than an old friend.

"His sister lives out on Log Town Road so he must be staying with her." He pondered this for a second when there was a chorus of friendly cries from many in the room. All eyes had turned to the television where the Power Ball numbers were about to be announced. Suddenly Jolly wished he'd bought a ticket, but his thoughts were drowned out by the excitement from the weaving men holding their tickets behind him.

"If I win, I'm gonna buy me a new asshole. All mine does is shits or bleeds all the time!"

"I'm gonna just enjoy my golden years."

"Hell, piss is golden."

"So's this beer!"

After all the prospective millionaires were brought back down to reality, Joanie asked Jolly a question.

"You heard about the break-ins lately?"

"No, that's news to me." Jolly had kept his own break-in and run-in with Snap to himself.

"You know I talk to the deputies all the time when they stop in for coffee, and they were talking the other day about several reported break-ins recently. They said they're looking for whoever done it."

"Did they say if they had any ideas who it might be?"

"If they did, they didn't say."

Jolly stubbed out his cigarette, hitched up his jacket, straightened his hat, and stood up to go. "I'll keep my ears open. Let me know if you hear anything, will you? And don't hesitate to call if you have any problems and need some help."

"I will, thanks Jolly." She looked deep into his eyes for a moment, gave him a smile, and headed back down the bar.

Chapter 12. Muddy Lanes

All through January and February, Jolly kept his
ears open for any news about Snap or Trick, break-
ins, drug activity, or any other strange doings in the
area. Lately, he found himself frequenting Maynard's
more than usual, and his warm friendship with Joanie
continued to heat up. Though they had never met outside
of the bar, the possibility was always there. Jolly took to
taking his meals sitting at the bar instead of in his old
booth so they could visit. She was still with her husband,
but she was also still not wearing her wedding band,
at least not at work. This both excited and disturbed
him. Living in such a small community, any marital
impropriety would go unnoticed for about two seconds.
He knew he had to take this slow and watch his step lest
he cross a line that he might later regret crossing.

Right after Christmas, the weather turned colder,
the ruts froze, and black ice formed on the mountain

roads. The week of New Years, Jolly helped Floyd
Boggess kill and butcher two hogs over at Floyd's place.
It was perfect hog-killing weather with the ground frozen
solid. Jolly hated butchering hogs in the mud. Jolly's
brand-new duck brown insulated overalls and blanket-
lined jacket looked shiny side by side with Floyd's faded,
old, ripped up insulated coveralls. Floyd decided to skin
the hogs this time instead of scalding and scraping the
hides. So, after shooting them near between the eyes
with a .22 Magnum, and slitting their throats to bleed
them out, the hogs were hoisted one by one in the
bucket of the tractor over to the barn and the homemade
gambrels. Floyd raised the bucket so Jolly, standing on
an old wooden ladder, cut through the hind legs and slid
the gambrels through the tendons.

They worked on the two hogs simultaneously
starting at the hind legs. After making a circular cut
around the leg below the hanging tendon, they worked
their way down toward the torso. Dark and dirty on the
outside, with long wiry hairs, and slick and greasy on
the inside, the skin began to hang downward as it was
removed. Each man, wearing a pair of leather gloves,
worked his sharp curved skinner blade expertly along,
careful not to remove too much fat or damage the bacon.

Floyd spit a dark stream of tobacco juice on the carpet
of frozen mud, manure, and straw as he mentioned he
heard that Trick Deihl was down in Florida somewhere.

"He ain't supposed to leave the state 'cause he's on
probation, but his probation officer lets him check in by
phone. He's lazy as hell and never checks up on anybody.
He's so lazy he'd shit in the bed and kick the turd on
the floor. When my sister's boy was on probation, hell,
he drove all over the country and that bastard never
checked in on him. "

"What the hell's Trick doin' in Florida, 'rasslin'
alligators? "

"I heard he got on a hot-tar roof crew. Winter's the
time for roofin' down there."

The skinning finished, Floyd loaded up the heads,
hides, and entrails in the bucket and dumped them over
the hill for the coyotes. They left the naked, headless
beasts hanging overnight to be butchered the next day.
Though Jolly was happy to help Floyd out just as a friend,
Floyd paid him with four dozen fresh eggs, several jars
of home-canned beans, and pickles from his garden,
and half a box of 30-30s. Floyd also promised Jolly some
sausage once he processed the pork.

By March, the land had thawed enough that the

frozen ruts on the farm were muddy lanes. Jolly walked along in his muck boots, his hands in the side pockets of his jacket, thinking about Lori. He needed to give her a call, see how she was, and try to find out what Snap was up to. He walked over to a large outbuilding he used for storing some of his equipment. As he dragged on a smoke, he noticed that one of the uprights holding up the porch was nearly rotted out. He made a mental note that he would have to replace it fairly soon. This was one of the older buildings on the property, and as he reached in his pocket for the key to unlock the door, he was reminded of something else. When Snap broke into the house and stole from him, it wasn't the first time had had been a victim of theft that year. Back in late summer, someone had poached a good bit of ginseng from his property. The ginseng came to mind because this was the building where he used to always dry out the 'seng he would harvest.

The ginseng season begins in September when the red berries that contain the seeds are ripe. An ethical 'seng hunter always plants the red berries on the spot where the ginseng root is dug up so there will be more ginseng there the following season. It requires a license, and digging the root out of season is a crime. When

dried, the root can bring in well over five hundred dollars
a pound depending, sometimes as high as eight hundred.

Last season when Jolly went out to dig 'seng on
his property, he found most of it had been dug up prior
to the season, sometime in August, before the berries
were ripe. The thief was not only robbing Jolly, but he
was also robbing future generations of harvesters by not
replanting ripe berries. Jolly had heard that dope-heads
had been poaching 'seng, drying out the root, and then
trading it for pills or other drugs. He couldn't help but
wonder if Snap had been the one stealing his ginseng.
Now he really wanted to call Lori and ask about Snap.
Thinking of Lori reminded him of another phone call
he had made years ago, not long after she had been
attacked.

After Jolly had inspected the damaged upright on
the porch of the building, he headed back to the house,
sat down on the chair on the porch, and eased his
heavily stockinged feet out of his muck boots. As he
entered the kitchen, he set the dirty boots down on an
old rubber mat by the door and proceeded to make some
instant coffee. Sitting at the kitchen table with a cup of
coffee in hand, he closed his eyes and recollected on
the call he had made all those years ago to the sheriff's

office. The deputy who answered the phone put him
through to the sheriff.

"Hey, Jolly, what can I do for ya?"

"Sheriff, I was just wondering if y'all have made any
progress on my niece's case."

"Well, Jolly, first of all, we haven't forgotten about
her. I promise you we've been workin' on it. It may not
seem that way sometimes, but we have. Now, second, it's
a screwed-up situation. We thought we'd have it solved
by now 'cause of the DNA we collected at the scene. In
fact, we had DNA from one of the other girls as well.
Remember that happened over a very short period of
time and we sent all of that DNA evidence together on
one trip down to Charleston. Then two things happened
that screwed us up good. The vehicle transportin' the
evidence was in a wreck on 77 north up from Lewisburg.
Now none of the evidence was destroyed but when it got
to Charleston that was the real problem." Jolly listened
patiently as the sheriff's story ruined his hope of finding
Lori's attacker anytime soon. "So, the evidence gets in
the hands of the state serologist over at the state crime
lab, and he turned out to be a crook. Remember that
crime lab specialist that the feds busted a while ago who
lost his license and got locked up for falsifyin', tamperin',

and destroyin' evidence? Well, that was him, and the D.A. told us that between the car wreck transportin' the evidence and this quack handlin' it, that nothin' will ever stand up in court. So, basically, we're back to square one. I hate to tell you that but that's just the way it is, and there's just nothin' I can do about it. We're just gonna hafta solve this one the old-fashioned way---without the DNA."

Jolly, at that time, had forgotten about the crooked doctor at the crime lab. He was disappointed but not surprised. He hadn't expected any good news from the sheriff anyway. He opened his eyes again, returned to the present and dialed Lori's number.

Lori sounded tired when she answered the phone.

"Hey Uncle Jolly, how're you doin'?"

"I'm doin' great. Just thought I see how you're doin'."

"I've been fine, glory to God, my job has been going good. I need a little work done on my house, but other than that I am well."

"Can you get Snap to help you out on the house?"

"Well, he's been down in Florida for a while. Says he's got a job roofing or working on houses or something like that."

"Well, that's great that he's working. I hope he's been keeping his nose clean."

"He says he's been working with an old friend of yours. Rick, or Dick…"

"Trick."

"Yeah, that's it, Trick. Well, anyway he sounded happy last time I talked to him."

"That's good to hear honey, I am sure he'll do well down there. Let me know; maybe I can help you out on the house."

The conversation with Lori was all Jolly needed to know. Snap was in with Trick Deihl, which was not a good prospect. Hot-tar roof work was not pleasant even in the cool months. Jolly had a feeling they'd both be back by summer. By then, he'd be ready for them.

Chapter 13. Lonely Day

Joanie switched on the lights at Maynard's as
she walked through the door. It was 4:00 am, and they
opened at 6:00. Her co-workers would arrive in an
hour or so, and she cherished the early morning quiet
and alone time each day. The work took her mind
temporarily off her troubles, principally her marriage.
After dumping the cold deep-fryer grease into the
gummed-up 55-gallon drum outback and refilling
the fryer with three gallons of fresh vegetable oil, she
cleaned what was left of last night's dishes and then
began prepping for the day. She placed two pans of
bacon into the large industrial-sized oven and began to
slice potatoes, throwing the slices into a huge cast iron
skillet whose permanent home was on one of the larger
burners on the gas range. With the potatoes frying, she
quickly moved from the kitchen to behind the bar and
took stock of the beer. After restocking the longnecks and

chucking the cooked potatoes into a large stainless-steel pan, which she covered with aluminum foil, she swept the small area of carpet in front of the bar and then took out the trash.

When she walked back through the door with the empty trash, she could hear the television set over the bar. She knew her co-worker Joyce had arrived. Joanie liked to work in silence, but Joyce's arrival was always accompanied by the switching on of the T.V. Every morning like clockwork, the old crone walked through the door with the same greeting, "Shitty-ass weather." Be it rain, wind, hot and humid, cold and frigid, it was always the same "shitty-ass weather" to Joyce. Joanie had heard it so many times that she didn't even notice it anymore. The good part of Joyce arriving each day was that was about the time that Joanie was able to take her first little break before the morning rush.

Nursing a cup of coffee, she threw on her jacket and stepped out back into the cool morning. The dark, hilly horizon was beginning to show signs of life as the eastern sky began to lighten. The slow rise of the distant sun summoned the songbirds who began their chirping to welcome the day. While listening to the unseen songsters, Joanie smoked and thought about her situation.

It seemed trouble was entering her life from several directions. For one, her marriage to Jerry was not in a good place. It was as if she suddenly found herself, after all these years. living with a stranger. He just wasn't the same man she married all those years ago. He had always enjoyed a beer or a stiff drink, but lately, it seemed that all he did was drink. He passed out early each evening and, if he didn't stop, she was certain that he would lose his job. It wasn't like he made a hell of a lot of money, but it was more than she made, and they couldn't make it on just one paycheck. Deep down, she still wanted him and needed him, but at the same time, she was losing hope and patience with him. She also wasn't sure just how much he needed her. She couldn't remember the last time he had been at all romantic with her, or even fun to be around. He wasn't receptive to her asking him what was wrong either. He just wasn't the same man. She didn't know why, and she didn't know what to do about it.

At the same time, she was troubled about Jolly. She really thought she was falling in love with him. He had always been around and had always been a nice guy, but lately, they had really clicked. He was just such a decent man and a real man. She knew he was attracted to her, and she liked it. He was older than her, but that wasn't an issue. He had his shit together, and that meant a lot to her. Working in a beer joint for as long as she had, she could weed out the bullshitters in a hurry and Jolly was no bullshitter; he was the real deal. Jerry, on the other hand, was lately something else. Her private time came to an end when the headlights of several trucks angled into the lot out front. She stamped out her cigarette on the gravel and headed back inside to the smell of bacon, biscuits, and hot coffee and the morning banter of hungry men and sassy women.

Chapter 14. Hop Light Ladies

As much as Jolly loved the stark beauty of the mountains in the fall with their Indian-corn hues of yellow, reds, and browns, he also loved the early spring. Mid-April found him in the mountains digging a mess of ramps to season his fried potatoes or fresh trout. The last weekend in April was the annual ramp feed at Maynard's and the public was welcome to bring in their own trout to throw on the big outdoor grill that was set up under a large portable awning in the gravel parking lot.

Jolly started the day well before dawn, heading up to Shaver's Fork with a lightweight spinning rod. There were other trout streams close by, but his favorite was up on Cheat Mountain, the highest-elevation trout stream east of the Rockies. As he drove down the old railroad bed, he passed a father with two boys. He slowed down and with his elbow hanging out of the window asked about the fishing. The boys answered by holding up a stringer of several rainbows and one golden trout. He gave them a happy thumbs up and drove on. His favorite spot was not accessible by vehicle. He parked by the road and set out on foot to a small tributary that was one of his best-kept secrets. Unlike the stocked trout the boys had caught that morning, Jolly was after some natives. He used a combination of woolly worms, night crawlers and wax worms until he got results. The small ones he returned to the stream to grow and prosper; the larger ones were his reward.

By eleven he had his limit of trout in the cooler, and he headed for Maynard's. The smoke from the grill was drifting upwards as he parked his truck and headed over to the awning with his trout and a large zip-lock bag of freshly cleaned ramps. The cook accepted both with a smile and added the trout to the grill and laid the ramps out on a large cast iron griddle set over low heat to slowly steam and cook the ramps to perfection. An additional propane stove was set up where several men were frying large portions of potatoes and ramps as well as bacon in huge skillets. Jolly bought a beer from the outdoor vendor and walked inside.

He took his usual seat, and Joanie came over wiping down the bar.

"Hey, how'd it go?"

"Got my limit, and I brought a gallon of ramps. Can't wait till it's all ready."

"The food should all be ready soon, then at 1:00 we got a fiddle band from Greenbrier County gonna play on the big flatbed trailer out in the lot."

"Sounds good. How've you been?" She leaned back against the counter behind the bar in front of the mirror and nursed a long neck. When she spoke, her words sounded thick in her throat, as if she might break down.

"Well, Jerry and I had a big fight last night. I swear, Jolly, I really do love him but sometimes he just drives me nuts!"

"What'd y'all fight about?"

"Same ol' shit. Him comin' home late. He's been out at his buddy's camp over on the Greenbrier so much lately, that I just told him he might as well just move in over there. And he's been drinking a lot lately, which worries me because he didn't use to do that. I mean he'd have a few beers now and then, but he was never a boozer." She finished her beer, threw the bottle into the large rubber trash can nearby and lit up a smoke. "And who am I to talk? I mean, I work in a beer joint, right? I may serve drinks all night, but I don't come home

smashed all the time. Something's going on with that
man, but I can't figure it out right now."

"Well, maybe he just needs some space or
something. None of us are perfect. Hell, I can't say too
much about it, my wife up and left me high and dry years
ago. Do you have to work in here all day, or can you work
outside?"

"Oh, I'll be outside just as soon as the food's ready."
She slipped him a fresh beer on the sly and gave him a
warm smile. "Why don't you go out and enjoy yourself?
I'll be out in a bit."

People were already lined up for the ramp feed
when Jolly walked back out into the sunlight. It was a
beautiful spring day. His flannel shirt and old canvas
hunting coat were just right to cut the cool mountain air.
He grabbed a paper plate and got in line with everyone
else. Fresh trout, fried potatoes with ramps, bacon, and
a small bowl of brown beans and cornbread made for
a perfect meal. Families sat elbow to elbow at the long
tables set up on the edge of the lot. Jolly ate his meal
and had some casual conversation with several people
he knew at the table. Before long Joanie was standing
behind a large pair of coolers selling beers, water, tea,
and soda. She waved and smiled at Jolly as he looked

her way. He answered by saluting her with his long neck. Two uniformed deputies sat and enjoyed their meals at the far end of the table as well.

Not long after Jolly finished his meal, the band had assembled and were ready to play. The fiddler kicked it off with "Hop Light Ladies," joined immediately by the clawhammer banjo, guitar, and a dog-house bass. Some people buck danced near the stage while most sat and just enjoyed the fiddle tunes. The living tradition of mountain music that has been and still is passed down from one generation to the next was on full display in the parking lot at Maynard's. The music made Jolly a bit nostalgic; he used to play guitar for square dances when he was younger. At one time he knew how to accompany all the fiddle tunes, and part of him wished he had his guitar with him right there, but he also knew how long it had been since he had played with a fiddler. His fingers had just enough arthritis to make such an endeavor painful and his chops were too rusty to keep up anymore. He instinctively began to tap his foot under the table as the band played "Three Forks of Reedy," a tune he hadn't heard in years.

Jolly decided to hang back from the gathering when he noticed Jerry's truck pull up. He slipped around behind the cab of his truck for a smoke where he could watch Jerry through the windows and not be noticed. The muddy tires and dried mud along most of the vehicle meant he had probably come from the fish camp. Two other men stepped out of the extended cab pickup and the whole lot looked none too sober. Among the three of them they were dressed in camo pants, dirty blue jeans, and overalls, with a flannel shirt or hunting jacket and muddy boots. Though he would have preferred to just leave, he felt a sense of protective loyalty to Joanie and wanted to be there to watch her back in case Jerry got violent.

Jerry was not an unknown quantity to Jolly. Jolly had been his supervisor at the State Forest the summer Jerry graduated high school. He had picked up a summer job and worked with Jolly every day for several months. When he thought about it, Jerry was probably dating Joanie at the time; Jolly might have even met her a time or two back then, but he didn't remember. He had found Jerry to be a hard worker but also a bit a pain in the ass who didn't always take direction well. Since that time, he had seen Jerry now and then around town. They were always cordial but never close. What Jolly did not know was how much Jerry knew about his

burgeoning relationship with Joanie. Surely word had
probably gotten back to Jerry by now that Jolly Taylor
was spending a helluva lot of time courting his wife
from a barstool at Maynard's several nights a week. One
thing was for sure, jealousy and alcohol don't mix well
together. Hopefully, there will not be a scene, thought
Jolly, so he stood by his truck and watched.

He saw the three men get in line, get plates and
sit together at the table closest to where Joanie was
working. She left her station, brought Jerry a beer, and
sat down beside him. Jerry chugged half of the bottle,
set it down and began to shovel in the food. Judging by
his actions he was pretty drunk. Joanie said something
to him, and the two other guys started to chuckle. This
set Jerry off, and he raised his voice a bit. Jolly couldn't
make out what was said, but it caught the attention of the
two deputies sitting at the next table. Joanie got up and
returned to her beer coolers. A few minutes later when
Jerry and his friends approached their truck, they were
greeted with two husky badges and a breathalyzer test.
The deputies noted the number of empty beer cans in
the cab and had each man blow into the machine. None
of the men were deemed fit to drive and all got a free ride
to the station.

The sun was beginning to set as Jolly walked over to where Joanie was cleaning up and preparing to shut down the outdoor drink stand.

"You okay?"

"Oh, I'm fine. Other than the fact that my drunk husband publicly humiliated me in front of the whole town."

"What was he mad about?"

"Alcohol just changes his whole personality and not for the better. He said he wanted to know where my boyfriend was, and what was I doin' hanging around an old man like Jolly Taylor."

"Well, maybe I just oughtta not come around for a while. Let him cool off, I mean, you two are married. Hell, I am too for that matter. Want me to go talk to him, tell him...tell him that we're just good friends and that nothin's goin' on?"

"I don't think that's a good idea. He won't believe you anyway."

"You know I love you Joanie, I just can't help it. You've just really got to me these last few months. Now I'm gonna make myself scarce for a while. You got my number; call me when you want to talk. It's easier to talk on the phone than in the bar with other people around

anyway. Let's see if Jerry changes his tune a bit when he
gets out of the hoosegow, and we'll just play it by ear."

She had started to cry a bit and was trying to
hide it; her eyes were watery and her voice thick with
emotion. "I love you too. Thanks, Jolly; I'll call you soon."
She hugged him tight for a moment, pressing her hard
breasts against his chest, and he held her. The heady
aroma of her perfume smelled good, and she felt good.
The thought ran through his head that with her husband
locked up she could come over tonight, and they could
finally be together, but then he knew that would just
complicate matters. He still felt awkward about being
in love with a married woman. He squeezed her tight
and without thinking gave her a quick kiss on the lips
and then left. She watched him walk off and get into his
truck. She waved as he drove off down the road and
around the bend.

Chapter 15: Blue Jay

Jolly stayed away from Maynard's and between work and chores around the farm managed to keep himself busy. He got a little lonely in the evenings after spending so much time at Maynard's. There was little if any radio transmission, and he didn't watch television. He had to get used to cooking his supper again. His diet gradually evolved from the usual cheeseburger and fries from Maynard's to anything from a can of sardines washed down with beer to eggs and fried boloney sandwiches. After supper he often took a walk around the property with Loop and then read for a while, often ending up in the rocker on the porch smoking and thinking of Joanie until he was ready for bed.

He never saw it coming, but he had to admit he was smitten with her and the chemistry they had together could not be denied. As brief as the moment had been, he couldn't forget the feeling he got inside when he held

her. Their relationship awakened something inside of
him that had been asleep for a long time. The human
touch is powerful, and it had been many years since
he had felt totally human. He found that he could not
keep her out of his thoughts. Everything he thought or
did eventually came back to her. Since he fell in love
with Joanie, life began to feel new and exciting again, a
prospect that he never thought possible.

One Saturday he finally decided to do something
about the rotten post that was holding up the porch of
the outbuilding. After a skillet of bacon and eggs with
fried potatoes and ramps, he put on his old work clothes
and headed out to the barn. He made several trips to
his truck until it was loaded with what he needed and
drove down the muddy lane and across the field to the
old shed. He pulled an old, long, grey oak board out of
the truck. It was one of many he had stored in the barn
that had been cut at the local mill years ago; the patterns
from the circular saw blade were still visible on the side
of the slightly frayed wood. He then cut about a six-inch
notch at one end of the board with his chainsaw and
placed the notch under the edge of the porch near the
rotten post while jamming the other end of the board
into the soft ground. The notched board would hold the

weight of the porch so the old post could be removed. He then pounded the post sideways with a hammer, at both the top and bottom, until the nails began to loosen and give-way, and then wrenched the post away from the overhanging porch.

Several years before, Jolly had cut down two tall poplar trees on his property among a large poplar grove. The grove trees were all very straight and tall and the two he chose were just the right diameter for porch posts. He had harvested them in the spring when the sap was running, which made it very simple to cut them to length and peel the bark. All he had to do was make a cut with his pocketknife at one end and the bark practically peeled itself with a gentle pull. He ended the day with several porch posts cut to length and a pile of curled up poplar bark, gray and rough on the outside and slick and shiny on the inside. The porch posts were then stored in the loft of the barn to dry and wait until they were needed.

He pulled the lightweight seasoned post out the bed of the truck, set it up where its predecessor had stood, made pencil marks, and began. A nip here and there with the chainsaw along with a small staircase style notch on the top to fit the overhead beam, and it was ready to be nailed in place. He noticed as he nailed in the new post that one of the old nails he had removed must have gone back many generations for it was an ancient homemade nail pounded out on an anvil. No doubt some Taylor ancestor had forged this nail back in the faded recess of time long forgotten. Jolly decided it was time to retire the nail from future service. He examined it in his fingers, twirled it around once or twice, and slipped it in his pocket.

He drove back to the barn and unloaded his chainsaw and other tools and began to think of lunch. Since he wasn't going back to Maynard's, he figured a boloney sandwich or maybe a grilled cheese sounded good. After storing the tools and shutting up the barn, he heard Loop give a light yelp, which was unusual for the dog. He scanned the grounds and caught a glimpse of Loop in the tall grass beyond the old pump. "Loop! What are you doin' boy?!" Loop came loping over and Jolly could see he had something in his mouth. "Give it here!" Jolly squatted down and held Loop's collar in his left hand and reached into his mouth with his right, his fingers negotiating the dog's clenched teeth. Then suddenly Loop seemed to lose interest. His jaw went slack and released his prey. Jolly felt slimy, wet feathers,

and looked down at what was in his hand. It was a dead
blue jay. An uncomfortable feeling came over him as he
recalled his early childhood and how his grandfather
had told him that killing a blue jay was bad luck. "Bad
medicine" is what he called it. Jolly deposited the carcass
in the field and couldn't shake off an air of trepidation and
foreboding that soured his mood for the rest of the day.

Chapter 16. Trick

Summer arrived and the lush green mountains seemed to bask and glow in the sunlight. A drive along the winding two-lane through Taylor Meadows was never boring in summer. The views of the countryside would morph from open fields with mountains in the distance, on a high flat ridge scattered here and there with old farmhouses, modular homes, or trailers, to a claustrophobic tunnel with the dark green forest closing in on both sides. Occasionally a wide spot in the road allowed for a pull-off that revealed a breathtaking scenic overlook that could, for a moment in time, hypnotize the viewer with an endless wave of green and eventually dark to fading blue ridgelines piled one upon the other into the hazy horizon. The high elevation ensured that, even in high summer, the thermometer rarely rose above eighty degrees.

Bright colors emanated from the large planters

that hung from many of the deep shaded porches on the houses along the main road. Small flower gardens blossomed with peonies and other perennials while lazy fat bees, hummingbirds, and dragon flies, or snake doctors as some called them, floated and hovered among the fragrant petals. Behind many of the homes were large gardens with rows of beans, peppers, greens, and maybe a patch of green corn, all of which were surrounded by sturdy fences to keep out the deer and rabbits.

Under the bright sunlight, with the cacophony of rasping insects the only sound on a lazy day in late June, Trick Deihl walked down the main drag about two miles from Log Town Road. He got back to town a week ago, and his older sister, a widow and retired cook at the local elementary school, allowed him to stay at her house. Sometimes she let him use her Subaru; sometimes he had to walk. Trick didn't mind walking, it gave him time to think, and he missed the cool summers in the mountains, especially after being down in Florida. He had gotten out just in time. There was no way he was going to stay down there roofing in the summer. At 63 years old he was too old to work in that deep southern heat like he could when he was young. At least he had earned a little money, but he planned on making more as soon as Snap got back. Snap had hooked up with a Cuban woman and decided to stay down south a while longer. Trick knew it wouldn't last, and he expected Snap back in the next few weeks when his money ran out.

The drivers who occasionally passed and gently waved at Trick as he walked down the road caught a quick glimpse of a rather menacing-looking figure. He was an older rough-looking character in a bright orange sleeveless shirt with large arms and a bit of a pot belly wearing an oversized straw cowboy hat and thrift store blue jeans slowly walking in the other direction. The drivers passing by would not have noticed the worn Velcro tennis shoes, lack of teeth, nut brown skin, and crude tattoos on both forearms, and a large lock back knife that hung from his belt in a snap sheath.

He had once been a dependable honest man before his life got hijacked by drugs and alcohol. He hadn't planned on his life turning out the way it did. One thing led to another as he had slowly developed bad habits, and one day he woke up a different person. That different person was one who felt no compunction about breaking the law or committing harm to others. He had somehow lost his moral compass over the years. He was raised to know right from wrong, he just preferred to choose wrong.

He was grateful to his sister for letting him stay
with her, and he did what he could to help her out with
trips to the store or doing odd jobs around the house.
He kept his drinking to a minimum in her presence and
never smoked in the house. He was also grateful that
his ragged trailer on Old Log Town Road was still there;
that had become his hiding place, his alone place. He
was pleased to find that it had been undisturbed while
he had been in prison, and the few things he had left
behind were still there though the place was a wreck. He
liked it that way, the better to discourage anyone who
might wander out there, though he couldn't imagine who
would.

Old Log Town Road was the leftover remnant of
what had once been known as Log Town back in the
days of big timber over a hundred years ago when nearly
the entire forest in the area was clear cut. Someone
named the place Log Town because at one time the
stacks of yarded logs rose higher than the surrounding
shanties, so it resembled a town of logs. After 1920
when the lumber boom ended, Log Town slowly began
to depopulate until it was just a rough road that led to
nowhere with a few isolated homesteads and little hope
for any future rejuvenation. Sometime in the 1950s a new

road was cut several miles from Old Log Town Road,
and it was given the uninspired name of Log Town Road.
This newer road was wider, more modern, and offered
better access to the community. Eventually Old Log Town
Road became a forgotten backwater where few lived
and fewer ventured. The dark-windowed buildings that
remained back there were soon overrun with multiflora
roses, sumac, blackberry vines, hornets' nests, and black
snakes. Trick's family had early roots in the original Log
Town and still owned some acreage and that was where
Trick had once put a small trailer.

Log Town had witnessed many nefarious deeds,
and the ground seemed haunted by its own history. More
than one man had been shot or stabbed there when
the place was overrun with wood hicks who would just
as soon hit a man as look at him. One of the adjoining
hollows was known for a large moonshining operation,
and the fruits of the stills fueled the loggers just as
much, or more, than the eggs and flapjacks they had for
breakfast each morning. If one ever crossed the area
with a metal detector, the harvest would include a rusty
mess of broken crosscut saw blades, and the ruins of a
portable band saw operation interspersed with the odd
wood stove, skillets, and the scattered rims of mason
jars.

Trick kept walking until he came to a small gas station where he always bought his cigarettes. He bought two packs, a lottery ticket, and a tall boy before heading back towards his sister's house. Tomorrow he could use the Subaru, and he would drive over to the trailer on Old Log Town. As he walked along sipping his beer, he thought of his plan make some money. He really wanted to get started tomorrow, but he had to wait for Snap to get back. One thing he learned in prison was patience. He would just do what he could to get things ready, and when Snap returned, slowly put his plan into motion.

The next day, Trick promised his sister he would get her some groceries; this enabled him to use the car. He set the grocery list on the passenger seat, checked his wallet for the money she had given him, and set off down the road. He would get the groceries on the way back; he had to stop by the old trailer first. Luckily, the Subaru had all wheel drive, or he may not have made it down the rough road. As the ruts were deep and the grass between the ruts was high, he had to take care to straddle them as much as possible. Snap's truck would be much better for getting in and out of this place. He reached the crest of a hill that was crowned with large, rotted out stumps of old forest giants. He parked the car just off the side of the beaten track.

The tall grass scraped against his jeans and slathered them with the thick morning dew as he made his way down the hill to the trailer. Before he approached the trailer, he picked up a large fallen branch, broke part of it off and carried it with him. He tapped the graying timbers of the small homemade porch with the stick checking for snakes. His footfall gently thumped on the hollow porch as he pushed aside an overturned plastic lawn chair and fumbled for the key. When he pushed open the door he was met by the dank, moldy smell of neglect and abandonment. His eyes slowly adjusted to the dim light that seeped through the dirty windows and he heard the scurrying of several rodents as he stepped into the narrow space.

He brushed aside hundreds of mice turds from the table, pulled up a chair, sat down for a moment and surveyed the interior of the trailer. There was no question that it was unlivable, but it was perfect for what he had in mind. This was where he had been living back when he was sent to jail seven years ago. The ceiling showed signs of water damage, and the whole place was a mess, but that didn't matter now; all he needed was something close by and isolated. He walked to the bedroom to the open closet door where he found a musty pile of old clothes and a plastic milk crate full of pornographic magazines. The bed, which had never been made, displayed a stained, bare mattress with old sheets and other bedding strewn across it here and there. The floor was littered with wadded up paper, beer cans, a few used condoms, and dirty t-shirts and underwear. Moving over to a chest of drawers, he noticed the bottom drawer held something he wanted; he laid the pistol out on the table and inspected it . Being a felon, Trick could not legally purchase a firearm, or own one. His recent release from prison was his second time around. He planned on getting a better gun through Snap once he got back, but until then this would do fine.

He had bought it at a flea market just after the first time he was released from prison after doing two years for burglary. It was a chance encounter, and he immediately grasped that it might be useful someday. The vendor had several antique and reproduction weapons for sale. The one Trick purchased was a modern version of an old design - a Ruger Old Army cap and ball revolver, a muzzleloading pistol. It was stainless steel and, when loaded properly, operated just as smoothly and effectively as a modern firearm. The purchase had two advantages for Trick: one, there was no record of the transaction, and two, it was not illegal for him to own a muzzleloader. The federal government did not require background checks for the purchase of muzzleloading and black powder firearms.

He had never loaded it or even shot it before, but that didn't matter. It was in good shape, had a 5 ½ inch barrel and felt good in his hands. When he bought it, he also picked up a box of caps, wads, a box of Speer .44 caliber roundballs, and an adjustable powder measure. He later got hold of half a pound of black powder, plenty for his purposes. He debated whether he should take the pistol back with him to his sister's or keep it here. He kind of wanted it around, but he also didn't want to overplay his hand and allow it to be seen by someone. If he ever did have to shoot anyone with it, his plan was to get rid of it immediately. Once they dug a roundball from a cap and ball out of someone's gullet, they wouldn't know what to think, and he was sure there would be no way to trace it back to him. In the end he decided to leave it at the trailer for the time being, but he decided to load it first.

He laid out six roundballs and six fibrous wads impregnated with lubricant side by side on the table. He then set his adjustable powder measure to hold 35

grains. Filling the measure, he tipped the revolver barrel
upward and rotated the cylinder. He then emptied the
powder measure into an empty chamber, placing a wad
over the powder followed by a bullet. A firm push with
the toggle on the plunger attached to the underside
of the barrel drove the ball home while slicing a razor
thin ring of lead from the roundball, which ensured a
tight fit and prevented the revolver from "chain-firing,"
or allowing fire from one chamber to spread to an
adjoining chamber and causing the cylinder to explode.
After repeating the process for the other five cylinders,
Trick placed percussion caps on the nipples and then let
the hammer down on one of the built-in safety notches
located between each of the capped nipples. He then
thought of a good place to hide the weapon. After looking
around for a minute, his eyes fell on the small microwave
oven on the dirty kitchen counter. If anyone broke in
this shithole, the last place they would look was inside
the microwave. So, he left the loaded revolver in the
microwave, ready in case he needed it.

Satisfied that the place would not be tampered
with in his absence, he prepared to head to the grocery
store. Before he left, he looked once more around the
trailer and ended up in the bedroom. He walked over to

a medium sized picture on the wall above the bedstand. After gently removing the picture from its hook and placing it on the bed, he removed a square piece of drywall that covered a little compartment. From the compartment he removed a small metal box and placed it on the bed. His eyes lit up as he opened the box and viewed its contents. It was all still there. For a moment, he relived the crimes that resulted in the contents of the box and the old fire in his belly returned. That was a long time ago, and it gave him a perverse pride that he had never been caught. After handling each of the items, he replaced them and returned the box to the cubby hole and replaced the picture on the wall.

At the store he bought what his sister needed along with a case of beer, more cigarettes, a loaf of bread, baloney, two boxes of generic cereal flakes and a gallon of milk for himself. He used his own money to buy his food. As he headed back for Log Town Road, he never suspected that he had been noticed by a passing vehicle on its way to Maynard's.

Chapter 17. *The Waltz of the Angels*

Jolly could hear the kitchen phone ringing as he stepped onto the porch upon returning from work. He made it in time to answer; it was Joanie. His heart began to speed up at the sound of her voice. She told him that Jerry was going camping again this weekend on the Greenbrier and that she was just lonely as hell and really wanted to come over. She had a tired, desperate-yet-determined tone in her voice as if she'd had enough, and either needed a change, or just didn't care anymore. She also told him that she called off work this Friday night. Since she called on a Wednesday, that gave him two days to get ready. He told her he would be home by 6:00 Friday evening and where to find the spare key. She said supper would be ready when he got home Friday night.

The next day after work, Jolly stopped by his friend's house and got his old Guild guitar back before stopping by the store for supplies for the weekend. He

had it all planned out, and the people who saw him
noticed that he walked with a renewed sense of purpose
had a lightness in his step. When he got home that night,
he flopped the heavy guitar case on the kitchen table and
found a new set of strings.

He hadn't played in a long time, partly because
he'd had no one to play for. He took his time removing
the old brown strings one at a time and replacing them
with shiny new ones. Using a tuning fork, he tuned the
new strings to the harmonic on the seventh fret of the
fourth string. He was pleased that he still had a good
enough musical ear to tune it. He wiped the guitar down
and shined it up a bit. The battered spruce top with its
sunburst finish was like an old friend to Jolly. He'd had
that guitar so long it truly was a part of him. He spent
the balance of the evening getting reacquainted with the
fretboard, the arthritis in his left hand preventing him
from properly playing some of the chords. He had to
switch out songs from C to D. The F chord was out as
well. From now on it was mostly D, A, and E chords for
him. His calluses were long gone as well and after a few
songs, he had to quit and let his fingers rest.

All day at work that Friday, Jolly was in a daze. He
went through the motions like a zombie with his mind on

Joanie. At lunch time, he drank his thermos of coffee and ate his sandwich in silence thinking of the night to come. He could barely contain himself at quitting time and had to force himself to slow down on the steep mountain roads and sharp turns that led him home. Then, finally he was home and there was her car, parked in his drive.

As he stepped onto the porch, he could hear music through the screen door. It was one of his old records, "The Waltz of the Angels" by Lefty Frizzell. He walked in to find the table set for two with a centerpiece of four, long candles, their yellow tongues of flame glowing upward. The evening sun shone through the window and set Joanie's auburn hair aglow, causing her hazel eyes to sparkle. He set his thermos on the counter and was immediately enclosed in her arms and pressed back against the counter. She hugged him as tight as she could and began to kiss him long and deep, her head shifting from side to side. As her large, warm breasts flatted out against his chest he returned her embrace and ran his hand down along her hips and squeezed her ass, slapping it several times. With each loud smack of his hand on her ass, she felt him getting hard against her belly and it was several minutes before their bodies parted and the months of pent-up desires, and unrequited passions abated enough for them to carry on a conversation.

"You found the old stereo." He said as Lefty Frizzell began singing "Long Black Veil."

"Yeah, my daddy used to have that record."

"It's one of my favorites; I haven't heard it in years."

After silencing him with a kiss, she gently took his hand and led him into the back room. Leading him over to the couch, she intently looked into his eyes as she unsnapped the buttons on her shirt and dropped it. Her large breasts hung low, her hard nipples welcoming his gaze. Before Jolly knew it her jeans were also on the floor, and he realized she had no panties. Her hands were at his belt and the weight of his wallet, keys, and belt knife caused his pants to fall to his ankles like lead. Her open hands pushed him back onto the couch and her arms wrapped around his neck with her breasts to his face, his pale, skinny legs shaking as she mounted him. She rode him hard, and they became true lovers. The slanted rays of the lowering sun stretched across the floor before they became two again.

He sat at the table while she brought him the supper of baked pork chops, green beans, mashed potatoes and gravy, and dinner rolls. She had canned the beans herself, and the mashed potatoes and gravy were all from scratch. She also brought out a bottle of red wine.

"I didn't know if you would want wine or beer with supper, so I brought both."

"Which ever one you want is good with me."

They decided on the wine. As they slowly ate, they realized that this was the first real time they had ever had to themselves, and it felt so good to be alone together. She told Jolly how she had seen Trick Deihl the other day as she passed the store. He was getting into a Subaru station wagon. Jolly nodded and told her that he knew Trick had been living with his sister on Log Town Road and that was her car. He soon changed the subject, not wishing to let talk of Trick intrude on the evening.

After the meal, Joanie brought out homemade peach cobbler and vanilla ice cream for dessert. Normally Jolly would have waved off any dessert after such a meal, but he couldn't refuse Joanie. She gave him a bowl of cobbler topped with ice cream.

"I like it with milk too."

"That sounds good to me."

She poured a little milk into each bowl, and they enjoyed the cobbler. Afterwards Jolly suggested they take a little walk before it got too dark. Hand in hand

---

they slowly walked across the property, Loop trailing alongside. He pointed out the buildings and explained the property line to her as she smiled and nodded in between stops for more hugs and a long kiss or two. She was quite at home and relaxed having grown up on a farm herself. They ended up back on the porch where they sat cuddled up like soulmates, gently swaying on the porch swing, watching the sun set over the distant ridgelines.

When they got back to the kitchen, Joanie collected the plates while Jolly disappeared into the back room.

"Now I've got something for you to listen to," he yelled to the kitchen as he fumbled with the record albums. When he returned, he was smiling and as she heard the slow lilt of the piano intro, tears welled up in her eyes as she reached for his hands. They slow danced together in the kitchen as Elvis's deep voice slowly and confidently sang, "Wise men say only fools rush in." As they held each other tenderly and gently swaying to the rhythm of the song, he whispered in her ear.

"I always thought that when you hear this song, the first person who comes to your mind is the one you truly love. Well, I'm seein' you in my mind right now."

"And I'm seeing you Jolly."

When the song ended, they continued holding each other for several minutes until he patted her rump to let her know the dance over. He led her over to the table and told her he had something special for her. She nodded and smiled, then teared up again when he returned with his guitar. He pushed his chair close to hers and looked deep into her eyes as he sang to her. His voice wasn't great; it wasn't trained, but the feeling was there and that was all that mattered. The tears streamed down her face as he sang her "Will You Lay with Me in a Field of Stone." She couldn't remember ever being courted so sweetly. She decided that Jolly was just the man she needed and that she just couldn't go back to Jerry after a night like this. He had planned on singing more songs for her, but that was enough. She didn't need another, it was perfect. He set the guitar on the table and took her in his arms.

"I love you, Joanie."

"I love you too, Jolly. That was beautiful. You are such a good man."

"And you're a good woman, the best I ever met. You know all those times I used to sit at the booth a Maynard's and you'd take my order and bring me my supper?"

"Yeah."

"Do you know what I was thinkin'?"

"What?" She broke into a broad grin.

"Just how much I'd just like to watch you take a shower sometime."

"Well ... since you were such a good tipper, we just might have to make that happen!" She laughed as she began to unsnap the buttons once again on her flannel shirt and kiss him at the same time.

The next morning Jolly got up early and cooked a big breakfast. He made homemade biscuits, and he knew just how much flour to put into the bowl to make six perfect biscuits. When the biscuits were done, he removed them from the oven and exchanged them for a baking pan of bacon on parchment paper. He then peeled two potatoes and cut them up into thin slices and fried them in vegetable oil until they were golden brown. After cleaning the skillet, he beat six eggs with some milk in a large bowl and poured them into the hot greasy skillet. Just as they were nearly done, he sprinkled cheddar cheese on the eggs and folded them over until they were ready.

He brought her breakfast in bed, and she sat up smiling and shaking her head in disbelief. No man had ever brought her breakfast in bed before. He laid down beside her and watched her eat. They talked about their situation and decided that they both had to seek divorces as soon as possible. In Jolly's case it was not a big deal; he and Eva had been separated for years, and she was probably expecting it anyway. Joanie's case was more delicate since Jerry lived nearby and he may not go along with the program. They would take it day by day and somehow work it out; new love late in life is never without baggage. Jolly also told her that he wasn't going to stay away from Maynard's anymore. There was no point staying away if they were going to be together from now on. He said she could keep the spare key, and he would have another spare made sometime soon.

Jolly took her dirty plate into the kitchen and over to the sink. He then filled the cast iron skillet with water from the tap and placed it back on the gas burner so he could boil the water and clean it up. He turned back to the sink where he had left the spatula and as he returned to the stove, he got a pleasant surprise. A laughing Joanie was suddenly on her knees before him tugging at his belt.

Chapter 18. *Up Jumped the Devil*

Trick Deihl was sitting in his sister's living room watching television when the landline began ringing. He heard his sister pick up the phone in the kitchen. She told him some man wanted to talk to him. The next morning Trick was dressed and ready, and at the appointed hour, a large, matte black pickup truck pulled into his sister's driveway. Trick hopped into the passenger seat, and he and Snap headed for Old Log Town Road.

It had played out just the way Trick thought it would. Snap had basically blown all his money on the Cuban woman, and it had gotten too hot to work. He put the phone number Trick had given him into his cell phone and, just as Trick knew he would, he called when he needed to make some dough. Rather than being tanned like Trick, Snap was red from sunburn, his fairer skin less tolerant of the sun . Trick just laughed when Snap

complained about how the cell phone he had bought
down in Florida wouldn't work up here in the mountains.
Soon Snap turned onto Old Log Town Road and before
long, they were parked and approaching the trailer.

Trick unlocked the door, and they went inside. He
left the door open to try and air the place out a bit to
remove some of the stale smell. They sat at the dirty
kitchen table, and Trick unfolded his plan.

"This is where I used to live about twenty years ago.
It's a mess now, but it used to be a half-decent place.
Anyway, it's perfect for what I got in mind. Now, there's
no electric or running water, so once in a while I need
you to bring in a couple of cases of water so we'll have
some while we're here."

Trick reached into his shirt pocket for his cigarettes
and set the pack on the table along with a folded sheet of
paper; Trick unfolded the paper and handed it to Snap.

"This here's a list of shit we need for this place.
We're gonna need a Coleman stove, propane—maybe
even a big propane grill would be better. Some propane
lanterns so we can see good, some flashlights—
headlamps would be best—look the list over. "

Snap held the paper in both hands and studied the
list as Trick continued.

"Now this is really important. First, you don't tell nobody about this place. Nobody, you hear? Nobody can know about this place; it's a secret. We can make a lotta money as long as nobody ever comes here but you and me. Which reminds me, do have a gun?"

"Yeah, I got a couple, a pistol and a shotgun."

"Good, I want you to keep one of them here with some ammo. We might need it. Oh, and add a shovel to the list. We may need one if somebody comes snoopin' around here."

Snap grabbed an old pencil from a jar on the counter and added to the list as Trick continued.

"We can make the meth right here. You made it before, right?"

"Yeah, couple times."

"Just be sure you don't blow the place up. Now, where are you stayin'?"

"I got a woman I know over by Elkhorn Ridge; I always stay with her when I am up here."

"Can you trust her? I mean you don't tell her nothin'. We can't afford to have anybody know what we're doin' or where we're doin' it." Snap nodded. "You got any idea where we could get a few more guns? I need one for myself, and I can't exactly buy one at the pawn shop."

Snap thought for a second. He knew Uncle Jolly had a whole gun case, but that didn't exactly work out last time. Maybe if they broke in together and Trick was with him, they could get what was in the gun case. He wanted to make Trick proud of him somehow; he never had a father figure in his life, so he told him.

"My uncle Jolly's got a big gun safe in his house, but..." Snap hesitated.

"But, what? You afraid a him?"

"Well, he is my great-uncle; he's always been good to me."

"Hell, I know who he is, I grew up with him. We played football together in high school. We hunted and fished; Jolly's always had a lotta guns. So, have you been to his place? Have you seen his gun safe? What kinda safe is it?"

"Uh, its green..."

"Green? Jesus Christ, you some kinda idgit? Is it one of those big-ass gun safes, or the little thin ones like they sell at Walmart?"

"Uh, I think it's one of the thin ones as far as I can remember."

"Ok, well, we'll plan that out later; we got time. What about ginseng? You know some good spots where we can snag some? We get it before the season, save it, then we can sell it later for cash or whatever we want."

"Yeah, actually my uncle Jolly's got some of that too. But I took a bunch of it last August, just like you just said, and I don't know if any of it's left. I just took it and run; the berries were green, and I didn't plant none of the seeds."

"Well, we'll look into that later too. Anything to make some damn money." Trick reached for his wallet, pulled out several large bills and laid them on the table.

"You take this money and start gettin' what we need on the list. Only buy what you have to; steal the rest wherever. Surely you can find a Coleman stove and lanterns around here, raid some fish camps. When you get the stuff, bring it here; I got an extra key for you. Just be careful nobody follows you, and don't make a habit of comin' out here too often; people around here are nosy. Which reminds me, and this is on the list, get some trail cams. Get at least two of 'em and set 'em up so's we can see the trailer, say one in on the front door and one around the side. If you can get three, that would even be better. You know how to set 'em up and check 'em and all that?"

"No problem. I've set up several."

"Ok, let's get goin'."

Chapter 19. A Thief in the Night

Within a week of their meeting in the trailer, Trick's scheme was put into motion. The talk at Maynard's was how people were beginning to miss things and how several fish camps on the Greenbrier had been vandalized. The thieves seemed to be taking propane tanks, camp stoves, cans of white gas, and anything else that was portable and of value. Joanie, who had moved in with Jolly, heard a new story nearly every day or so. When she told Jolly about it, he suspected that Trick had something to do with the thievery. Jolly had called Lori recently. and she had told him that Snap was back in West Virginia and "living with some woman on some mountain somewhere." When Jolly heard that Snap was in the area, he had no doubt that Snap was working with Trick Diehl, and whatever they were up to it was no good.

Several miles from Maynard's, Snap made his

way through the underbrush. He figured this would
be the last camp he would hit before reporting back to
Trick and getting the operation started. So far, he had
been pretty successful at stealing what he needed and
didn't have to spend too much of Trick's money. He had
gotten a hold of several trail cams from property where
he knew people had deer stands or hunted coyotes. He
had gallons of white gas and plenty of propane tanks,
both large and small. There were a couple of close calls,
but nobody had caught him, and he didn't think he had
been spotted by anyone. These thoughts poured though
his head as he approached the small board and batten
building with a long, low porch facing the river.

He stepped up on the porch and found a green
propane tank which was a good sign. Several empty beer
cans littered the porch and one empty bottle rested on
the rail. An old coffee can sat near a plastic chair, the can
full of cigarette butts and tobacco juice. A tangled mess of
monofilament lay like a rat's nest at the edge of the porch
and an old thermometer was nailed to the wall beside
the narrow door. The door was slightly ajar, and Snap
quietly opened it and stepped inside the darkened room.
The one window on the opposite wall was covered with
a blind. Two steps into the room and a sticky roll of fly

paper hanging from the ceiling stuck to his hair and face
causing him to reach out with his hands.

"What the hell!"

No sooner had the words left his mouth than he
heard the distinctive sound of a cocking revolver from
the dark corner of the room.

"Freeze, you asshole! What the hell you doin' here?
Who the hell are you!"

Snap began to shake and froze in place as he was
ordered to raise his hands in the air. Nasty yellowed fly
paper clung to his face. Then the window blind abruptly
slammed upward, and a flashlight beam blinded his eyes.
Jerry stepped out of the shadows with a .38 in one hand
and flashlight in the other. Jerry's shirt was damp from
sweat, and Snap could smell the liquor on his breath.

"Hey man, stay cool, I ain't stealin' nothin'."

"Then what the hell you doin' here? Friends a mine
been losing shit all over here lately. You the son of a
bitch's been stealin' from everybody? What you want our
shit for?"

Snap didn't have an answer, he just stood there
with his hands up and fly paper stuck to his eyebrow and
in his hair. "You mind if I rip this fly paper off my head?
It's grossing me out."

"Ok, but you're gonna tell me what you're doing here."

That night Trick got a phone call from Snap. He was very upset and needed to see Trick. Something happened and it was important. Trick told his sister he was going for a walk and headed down towards the main road. He waited a few minutes at the corner, smoking, when Snap pulled over and picked him up.

Snap was sweaty, dirty, and agitated. His face was filthy with some sticky substance and his hands were shaking.

"What's goin' on?"

"I got the stuff you wanted," Snap said. "I got propane, white gas, a bunch of different stoves, cooking pots, all kinda shit like that. And I got four trail cams, too."

"Ok, that's good, but what's goin' on? Something's botherin' you. Did somebody see you?"

"Well, the last place I hit there was this drunk idgit there, and he pulled a gun on me."

"Ok. Did you kill him, or what?"

"Hell, no I didn't kill him. He pulled a gun on me and, and ...."

"And what, goddammit?"

"And he made me tell him what I was doin' there, and he wants in. He says he wants a piece of the action."

"You're shittin' me!"

"I wish I was."

"All right, well we'll have to deal with it, tell me who he is."

Chapter 20. In the Devil's Den

Joanie brought Jolly another beer at the bar at Maynard's, and they each had a cigarette. Joanie told him the latest she had heard; for a community that had practically no internet, Maynard's was a gold mine of local gossip.

"Joe Sweeny was in today and said he saw your great-nephew Snap yesterday."

Jolly perked up with attention. "He did? Where?"

"Said as he passed the intersection, he saw Snap turning down Old Log Town Road. Everybody knows that dull black truck of his."

"It's Flex Seal. That's what he painted his truck with." Jolly smashed his cigarette into the ash tray. "Well, that's interesting; good to know."

As Jolly drove home that night all he could think about was Snap driving down Old Log Town Road. He knew Snap was going out to Trick's trailer. He had a good idea what they were up to, but he wanted to know for sure. He decided to slip out there and have a look around. He was still pissed at Snap for stealing from him; maybe Snap had stashed some of Jolly's stuff out there. Maybe he could find his pocketknives and grandfather's watch. It was a longshot, he knew, but just maybe he would find those things in Trick's trailer.

When he got home, Jolly made sure he had what he needed. He strapped on his .357 in an old Hunter holster he had laying around, got his mag-lite, his headlamp, and a crowbar. He switched into some camouflage hunting clothes, packed a water bottle and a couple of left-over biscuits in his pockets, and headed out. He had no intention of driving down Old Log Town Road. He knew a back way into Trick's trailer. It involved a little extra driving, but he knew just where he could park his truck, hike down the creek bed, cut through some fields and then up a hollow and he would come out behind Trick's trailer. It had been years since he had covered that ground in daylight and there was a real chance he could get lost, but his blood was up, and he felt he could make it.

After making his way through the darkness, he noticed the moon steadily rising. It was not as full as the other night, but it was enough to help guide his way. He

was careful to let his eyes adjust and used the headlamp
sparingly so as not to draw any attention to himself.
Then, after quite a while of tramping, he saw a reflection
up ahead through the trees. It was his flashlight
reflecting on the windows of Trick's trailer.

He immediately turned off the light and hunkered
down for a minute—watching and listening. He found
he was breathing heavily, and he could hear his heart
thumping in his ears as he waited to see if the trailer
was occupied. He took a drink of water and tried to
calm himself. The air temperature dropped, and Jolly
felt a chill. The spirits of the haunted ground of Old Log
Town were swirling around the trailer, on their nightly
tramp with the ghosts of murdered loggers and other
malevolent souls lost to moonshine and darker vices.
Directly he decided there was no one in the trailer, so he
rose and slowly stalked toward the back door.

As he neared the door, he was hit with the split-
second flash of a trail camera not fifteen or twenty feet
away. He stopped in his tracks and sweat began to
run down his back. That got him spooked, which was
something he had not expected. He swung his head
around and saw the little red glowing light that betrayed
the location of the camera. With the crowbar he removed

the camera from the tree and smashed it. If they were
really sophisticated, they might already have his image
on a computer, but he doubted it. More than likely, they
would have to retrieve the chip in the camera to view the
photos. He reapproached the trailer.

After forcing open the door with the crowbar, he
turned on the powerful mag-lite and shined in around
the interior walls. He was down the hall from the
kitchen, careful not to upset anything. He made his way
to the kitchen and looked around. When he saw a haul
of camp stoves, propane tanks, white gas cans, large
cooking pots, boxes of blue tip matches—he knew what
it was. He instinctively knew Snap and Trick were the
thieves everyone was talking about. He could also tell
that they hadn't started making any meth yet, but it could
start up any day.

Jolly shone the light around the bedroom. He was
disgusted, but not surprised at the mess. He looked in
the closet, opened a few drawers, and then he noticed
the slightly crooked picture on the wall near the bed. His
curiosity got the best of him, and he removed the picture,
only to find the cut-out square of dry wall. He pulled
out the piece of dry wall and set it on the bed. The small
metal box shone dull and shadowed in the glow of his

light. He carefully pulled it out of the cubby and set it on the bed. It opened with a small snapping sound, and Jolly stood transfixed for a few seconds. He could not believe what he was seeing. He dumped the contents of the box onto the soiled mattress and looked through the pile of jewelry and driver licenses. He immediately recognized his niece Lori's DMV photo from just over twenty years ago. There were licenses belonging to three other women as well, all young and about Lori's age. The box also contained rings, bracelets, necklaces, and other jewelry.

Jolly's mind was racing. He felt a rage slowly building inside him. He wanted vengeance, and he wanted it right now. He also didn't want to be in the trailer anymore; he needed to get the hell out of there, get his head together, and decide what to do. Now that he knew that a man he had once called a friend had raped his niece, a thousand thoughts were going through his head of what he wanted to do to Trick Deihl once he found him.

Jolly returned the piece of dry wall and replaced the picture on the wall but decided to just leave everything displayed on the mattress. He moved the bedding just a little so the artifacts could not be seen from the doorway. He figured Trick wouldn't notice anything was wrong for a while, and that might give Snap a chance to find it. Then he would know just what kind animal he had chosen for a partner. Retracing his steps, he set left the trailer and headed back the way he came confident that no one had seen him. What he didn't know was that there was more than one trail cam.

Chapter 21. Bad Blood

The next night Trick and Snap had a meeting at the trailer. After talking it over, Trick agreed to meet Jerry. He told Snap to go pick up Jerry and bring him along. Trick would be waiting with a gun and depending on Jerry's demeanor, it could go either way. Trick waited in the dark trailer, smoking and drinking beer. He would turn on the lanterns after Snap returned. On the table was Snap's shotgun, a single shot 12 gauge. Though he hadn't told Snap, he had also decided that Jolly Taylor had to die. Snap had shown him the grainy image of Jolly in full camo, carrying a crowbar or something, standing near the trailer. Trick just said that they would rob him like they had planned.

Eventually he saw the glow of headlights over the rise and then darkness. He heard two doors slam and he readied himself. He wasn't going to let some drunk fisherman ruin his plan. He saw the beam of a flashlight refract through the dirty window and then heard footsteps and voices on the porch. The door opened, and Jerry walked in followed by Snap. Jerry saw the shotgun pointed at him, and he knew these guys were serious. Trick told Snap to search Jerry for a gun. Snap said he already did, and Trick told him to do it again. Satisfied that Jerry was unarmed, Trick told him to sit down, still covering him with the shotgun.

"All right, who are you and what do you want?"

"My name's Jerry Collins."

"And what do you want, Jerry?"

"I, uh, I uh, just want in on whatever it is you guys are up to."

"And what is it that you think we're up to?"

"Well, you're makin' meth, right? I can help sell it for you. I work at the garage old Roger James runs."

"Out past the diner?"

"Yeah, you know it."

"But I don't know you. Why should we let you in? Why don't I just kill you right now?"

"Because I can help you sell it. I swear I won't tell nobody."

After some more negotiations, Trick decided he was just going to shoot Jerry and have Snap bury him.

He made Jerry think all was well and put him at ease. He passed Jerry a beer and they toasted each other across the table. Trick told Snap to light the lanterns so they could see better, and Snap had a question.

"Hey, Trick, what about that thing at Uncle Jolly's? We gonna do that tomorrow or what?"

Trick grabbed Snap's arm as a sign for him to shut his mouth, but it was too late. Jerry had heard the name "Jolly" and his whole demeaner changed.

"Did you say Uncle Jolly? You talkin' about Jolly Taylor?"

Snap looked at Trick and Trick gave him a look that demanded silence.

"Yeah, Jolly's Snap's great-uncle. What's that to you?"

"He's the son of a bitch who's been screwin' my wife. Hell, she's done moved in with him. If you boys got some plan to screw him over, I am in!"

It all happened the next day, while Jolly was at work. Joanie had slept late and was tinkering in the kitchen working on a homemade pie crust. She had to get some laundry done before she left for work at four. She heard the dull sound of an engine and tires on the gravel. Loop barked. Looking out the kitchen window, she saw Snap's dull black pickup heading up the driveway towards the house. She wondered what he wanted. He surely knew Jolly wasn't home. Then she saw the truck park, and Snap stepped out with two other men. It took her a second, but she recognized Jerry, and he had a pistol in his hand. Her blood froze as she saw them walking right up to the porch.

She ran to the front door, and slammed it shut setting the bolt. The sharp sound of Loop barking was answered with a single gunshot followed by a whining yelp. Her hands shook as she ran to the bedroom. Jolly had told her where he kept the 30-30 rifle. She used to hunt deer some years ago, so she knew how to use it. She opened the lever enough to see the base of a brass shell casing in the breech; the rifle was loaded. As she shut the breech and stepped back into the kitchen, she could hear pounding on the door, and Jerry's drunken voice screaming like a banshee.

"Come out you goddamn bitch! Where's your boyfriend? We gotta present for you bitch!"

What Joanie didn't know was that Jerry told Trick and Snap that they could both take turns with Joanie after he beat the shit out of her. Once Jerry beat her to his satisfaction, he was through with her. Whatever they did to her was none of his concern. Of course, Trick also wanted whatever was in the house; the woman was just a side dish.

Joanie could see Jerry's head peeping through the window at the top of the locked door as he kicked at it violently with his steel-toed boots. In his right hand he waved his .38. Trick and Snap were out of sight, probably off the side of the porch. The pounding and screaming continued, and Jerry's rage seemed unsufferable. Maybe they'll just leave, she thought, hoping she wouldn't have to shoot, but the pounding got louder, and Jerry's voice hoarser as the threats continued. Then she heard the wood on the door splinter as Trick stepped up on the porch, beside Jerry, and with a terrific ax blow, rived a long vertical crack down the door.

She realized the door would soon be breeched. Joanie cocked the hammer, raised the rifle and, looking down the iron sights beneath the raised scope mount, fired straight through the center of the door. She did not feel the recoil but felt the concussion of a high-powered rifle being discharged in an enclosed space and smelled the acrid scent of smokeless powder. The sound of Jerry's screams ended abruptly, and she heard a body slam onto the porch. She worked the lever, and the empty shell casing flew across the room and landed in the sink with a tinkling sound. Going to the window, she saw Trick and Snap scrambling to open the truck doors. She stepped out onto the porch, and saw Jerry laying at her feet, his eyes open and lifeless, a revolver in his clenched fist.

Then she heard the truck start up and begin to throw gravel as Snap punched it into gear and started to race away. She raised the rifle and, using the scope, shot a round at the truck. She saw dust fly where the bullet ricocheted off the top of the truck's cab. She heard the whine of the truck's engine as it took the curve at full speed, racing away. Then, there was just the silence of the country and a large cloud of gravel dust that seemed to hang in the air for minutes.

Joanie was shaking and found that she was clutching the rifle so hard, she had to sit down on the porch swing and use her left hand to help loosen the grip of her right from the rifle's wrist. Her body trembled. She set the rifle down on the porch, and then she saw Jerry, his body bloody and still. She was sobbing uncontrollably when she dialed 911 and reported what had happened. She asked the dispatcher to call the State Park and get a hold of Jolly and tell him the news.

Chapter 22. Bloody Porch

When Jolly got home, the yard was full of vehicles.
The sheriff had arrived along with several deputies and
state troopers. EMTs for the fire department were there
as well. Jolly jumped out of his truck and ran over to the
EMT vehicle searching for Joanie. Instead, he was told
she was inside with the sheriff and some troopers. When
he asked who was in the body bag, they told him it was
Jerry Collins, and that Joanie had shot him. Before Jolly
made it to the porch, he saw a deputy holding Loop in
his arms; the dog's eyes were rolled back, and a rime of
spittle ran from his grey muzzle. According to the deputy,
the dog had been hit with a grazing shot from a pistol.
He had suffered a gunshot wound to a hind leg but was
still alive. The EMT squad had given the dog a small
amount of sedative and bound his wound. Jolly placed
his head against Loop's sleeping face and whispered
to his dog. "You're a good boy buddy, you just tried to

protect us. You're gonna be okay." Then he kissed the old dog on the forehead and walked into the house.

Joanie was sitting at the table, a blanket wrapped around her, surrounded by law enforcement officials. Her eyes were swollen from crying, and she was still shaking. When she saw Jolly, she rose out of the chair and hugged him. She violently shook as her sobs reverberated through her body. Jolly held her as tight as he could and gently whispered to her. When she calmed down again, Jolly helped her to her seat at the table. The policemen were patient and polite, speaking to her in the hushed tones of men who have daughters.

For the next two hours, Joanie told her story several times to the officers. The sheriff told Jolly that he had to impound the rifle for the time being and asked if he had any other weapons for self-defense. Jolly told him he had a shotgun, and the sheriff tried to sound reassuring.

"Now I have to follow protocol. A man's been killed with a rifle. It was self-defense and justifiable homicide. An official investigation will have to be conducted, no question, but from my experience I would have to say that she'll be cleared of any malice. I am also going to recommend to the DA that no charges be filed in the death of Jerry Collins."

The sheriff promised to check in with them in the
morning and advised they should be vigilant in case
Trick or Snap somehow should circle back their way.
His deputies were scouring the county for the two
outlaws. The EMT squad told Jolly they would take Loop
to the nearest veterinarian and not to worry. They also
promised to call him as soon as they had Loop settled
in for the night. Jolly thanked them, shook their hands,
and said, "I sure hope you find them." He neglected to
mention that he probably knew where they were, at
Trick's trailer, but then he wanted to find Trick first.

Jolly made Joanie some coffee with brown sugar,
milk, and bourbon and led her into the bedroom. After
he held her for a good while, and she calmed down, he
told her he had to fix the door and would be nearby. He
took the small automatic pistol he kept in the glove box
of his truck and set it by her nightstand. She thanked him
and took another sip of coffee.

The first thing Jolly did was retrieve the Winchester
Model 12 shotgun from behind the seat of his truck.
He brought it into the kitchen, jacked out all the shells,
checked the breech, held the breech up to the light and
checked the barrel for obstructions. He then reloaded
it with 2 ¾ inch number 4 shot shells. After setting the

shotgun in the corner of the kitchen counter, he walked out across the lot to the row of old cars, reached for his keys, and popped open the trunk of the GTO. He pulled out the single shot 12-gauge shotgun that he'd had since he was a boy, an old H&R Topper. After grabbing another box of shells, he slammed the trunk and headed to the barn for some tools to repair the door.

By dark he had the door repaired and had checked all the other doors and windows in the house. Satisfied that his home was secure, he checked in on Joanie and found her finally asleep. He breathed a heavy sigh and opened the fridge for a beer. Then he took another and set two bottles on the table. His mind was reeling from different emotions. He was pissed off about those assholes trying to kill his woman and his dog and then rob him. He was afraid for Joanie and her emotional stability; after all, she did just kill her own husband, asshole that he was. He was concerned about how this was going to end, and with Snap being kin, it was a delicate matter which in turn worried him, but his hunger was winning out.

He searched the larder and grabbed a can of SPAM and a yellow onion. He poured some bear grease in the skillet and set the gas burner to medium heat. Soon the chopped onion and SPAM meat were sizzling in the skillet. He threw in a chopped-up potato as well and sprinkled all of it with black pepper and some Louisiana hot sauce. He drank the two beers while his meal cooked. After his meal, he drank another beer and, taking the shotgun from the kitchen, sat out on the darkened porch, and smoked for a while before turning in for the night. The light from the full moon cast silver light and blue shadows across the lot as he locked the kitchen door and crawled into bed with Joanie.

Chapter 23. *The Hole in the Wall*

Snap gunned it so hard leaving Jolly's farm that Trick slammed his head on the dash and almost flew through the wind shield. Trick yelled at him to slow down and control himself as he fumbled for his seat belt.

"Go to the trailer! We can hide out there tonight, and then we'll have to ditch this truck and steal some other vehicle. Whatever we do, I am comin' back and killin' 'em both!"

They made it to the trailer by taking winding side roads and walking in the back way, just as Jolly had done the night before. The truck was hidden off the road a good way so that it might not be found for a while. Both covered in dust and streaked with sweat when they reached the trailer, huffing and puffing along the way.

When they got inside, they sat at the kitchen table and chugged several warm beers and then lit up cigarettes.

"Damn, that Jerry screwed this whole thing up," said Trick, as if he had to blame someone for his failed plan. "She had more sand in her than I thought."

"No, shit. I ain't never seen no one get killed before."

"You get used to it after a while."

"Man, I need to crash for a while, my head is killin' me."

"Go crash on the bed, I got some thinkin' to do. And light one those lanterns and bring it over here."

Snap lit one of the propane lanterns and set it on the counter next to the microwave behind Trick so as not to blind him. Snap then went into the bedroom to lay down. He was gone a few seconds when he called out from the darkened room. "Hey, Trick, what's all this shit on the bed?"

"What shit?"

"I don't know, it feels like jewelry or something."

Trick walked in carrying a lantern and shone it over the bed. There splayed out all over the mattress were the fruits of his evil labor. The rings and other trinkets overlapped several shiny plastic cards with women's faces on them. "Hey, that's my mom!"

The muzzle flash from the heavy pistol lit up the dark room. Fire flew from the sides of the cylinder and ten inches out of the end of the barrel. The powerful concussion sent loose dust up from the carpet and down from the ceiling tiles. The heavy smell of sulfur filled the small room and the pall of white smoke hung over the bed and reflected the lantern light. Snap's brains covered the wall. His heavy, dead form bounced as it hit the mattress and some of the jewelry fell to the floor. The powder smoke resembled fog in the room as it silently dissipated. Trick slowly retrieved the jewelry and cards, replaced them in the small metal box, and put it all back into the wall behind the picture. So, Trick thought, if Jolly asks, I can tell him it was his fault that Snap was dead. If he hadn't meddled around in the wall and left my property alone, Snap would still be living.

Trick now knew that Jolly knew about Lori. He had to get to Jolly as soon as he could and prevent him from passing the word. If he knew his old friend as well as he thought he did, then it was certain that Jolly had not told the sheriff. Jolly was like him in a way; he liked to take care of things himself, and that was just fine by Trick.

Chapter 24. Sunup

It was sunup, and Jolly had his head resting on Joanie's breasts with his arms around her in the bed. The sound of her heartbeat and the heave and sigh of her breathing were warm, magical sounds to him. She was such a beautiful woman; he couldn't believe his luck falling in love like this at his age. And he could tell that she genuinely loved him too. He just couldn't ask for more. She gently rolled over and he was running his hand down across her buttocks when he heard a vehicle in the distance that sounded out of place. Then it started to get louder, an ATV he thought.

Tucking in his pants into his boots, he looked out the kitchen window and saw Trick Deihl heading across his field on a four-wheeler through the thick morning mist. So, here he was. He'd rather come after me and Joanie than try and run from the law. Jolly thought of Loop then remembered that the dog was safe at the vet.

He reached over to the corner of the counter, grabbed his shotgun, and walked out onto his porch. The morning sun was in his favor, and Trick would be squinting right into it soon if he stayed facing Jolly's porch.

They weren't there to have a conversation. Trick raced the four-wheeler right at the porch with Snap's single-shot shotgun cocked in his right hand. His arm was stretched straight out to fire when the four-wheeler skidded on a loose track of gravel and the weapon went off prematurely. By the time Trick had absorbed the recoil, he was hit with a blast from Jolly's pump gun. Jolly jacked another shell into the chamber and stepped off the porch slowly walking toward Trick's lurching body. Trick was on his back, his chest punctured through with the number 4 shot, still alive and trying to move his arms to his belt line. Jolly kicked him, rolled him over, and removed the cap and ball revolver from the small of Trick's back and flung it away.

Trick looked up at Jolly with black eyes of hatred. He knew he had lost the duel, and now, he was in Jolly's hands. Jolly disappeared for a moment and returned with a handful of bailing twine. Trick was hogtied when Jolly hauled him into the bucket of the tractor and headed over to the high field. The engine drowned out Trick's screams and pleas for mercy as they passed Turtle Rock, just below the old blackened firepit. In younger days, this is where they had gotten drunk in the moonlight beneath the stars with other friends, played guitars, and sung to their girlfriends. Stabs of immeasurable pain wracked Trick with each lurch of the bucket over the uneven ground. Then, Jolly heard a hellish scream as Trick saw what he knew was coming, the dark mouth of The Big Hole.

Jolly didn't want to hear the condemned man's last words, or offer him a cigarette, he just emptied the bucket into the large, ancient crack in the Earth and watched the mangled, bloody form disappear from the sight of man forever. He set the brake and made sure that Trick's shotgun and pistol were gone as well before heading back down to the barn. After he had rehoused the tractor and washed out the bucket, he drove Trick's stolen ATV up through the high field and dropped it down the hole as well.

It was 7:55 am by his wristwatch when Jolly walked back onto the porch and to the kitchen door where Joanie was waiting in panties and a t-shirt. She had Jolly's old single shot 12 gauge in her hands and tears running down her face. He gently took the gun out of her shaking hands, set it aside, and held her in his arms until the trembling stopped and the tears dried.

Made in the USA
Monee, IL
24 September 2024

65722572R10100